Christmas Treasures

Christmas Treasures

A Collection of Christmas Short Stories

KARLA AKINS
SUSAN F. CRAFT
ANNE GARBOCZI EVANS
LINDA S. GLAZ
KARLENE JACOBSEN
KAREN CAMPBELL PROUGH
CHRISTINA RICH
KATHLEEN ROUSER
DONNA HUBBARD SCOFIELD
JOANNE SHER
ELAINE STOCK
APRIL STRAUCH
KAREN WINGATE
PATTY WYSONG

Hot cocoa, Christmas cookies, and the smell of evergreens will help transport you to the lives of dozens of holiday characters. From unrequited young love, to a father who feels the need to help his daughter's love life, to a nursing home matchmaker, Christmas is in the air. Even in the life of a backwoods widower who must find hope under his tree.

Old loves, new loves, hoped for love. They are all wrapped and tied with a bow in this bundle of Christmas cheer. Baby Jesus in a pageant and Baby Jesus in the Temple, bringing the same message of hope, peace, and joy. Christmas is seen through a child's eyes as hearts are warmed with innocence and love, especially at the time of year when miracles seem more possible than ever before.

Put on your mittens, your hat and scarf, and step into a winter wonderland of giant flakes, chilly noses, foggy breath, and heart-warming stories. It's Christmastime. The most wonderful time of the year.

table of Contents

Part-time Job

LINDA S. GLAZ

Chapter One

Gwyneth tugged the toy bear to her chest and let the tears flow. How could she tell Isabella that Daddy wasn't going to be home for Christmas? Probably wasn't coming home at all. Missing. Taken from the civilian barracks at night. She choked remembering the news last night. What the extremists had done to that journalist. Had Brady been taken by…she shook curls from her eyes. No. No! He had to be all right. Somehow. Somewhere. Trying to get home to them.

She cuffed the stuffed animal right side the head and slid to the floor of Isabella's room with a thump. Taking the letter from her pocket, she stared at the words. Missing. How could a man just up and go missing? She hadn't wanted Brady to go to Afghanistan. Civilians didn't have the same force of the military behind them. Hearing the door close, she rushed downstairs.

"Mommy, can we make cookies? Mommy, what's wrong?" Round blue eyes met Gwyneth's gaze. "Mommy, you okay?"

Gwyneth pulled Isabella into a hug then rose with the wiggly little four-year old in her arms. "Where's Grandma?"

"She's bringing in chocolate chips for cookies. Yum."

"Hey, Button." She flicked the end of Isabella's nose. "We'll start the Christmas cookies today, too." Tears filled her eyes again, but she licked her salty lip and glanced away. No sense getting her baby in a tizzy.

A sweet smile and shining eyes met Gwyneth's gaze. "Cookies for when Daddy comes home, right?"

And then Gwyneth completely lost it.

Brady watched from a distance. He could walk…limp right back into their lives, but what good would he be? The fingers of his right hand clutched his left arm. Pinched at the end, where a forearm should be. *I want them in my life again, but I can't do it to them.*

Half a man. Half a husband, half a father. What kind of job would he have? He had trained civilians for overseas duty. How good would a one-armed limping man be in that field? He'd never be able to hold an M-3 carbine again. So no training job.

It was better to let his family get on with their lives. Mac had promised him he wouldn't tell anyone. Just let Brady fade away to some other life. Enough scrimping and he could live on part of his medical pension. As long as no one told.

"Brady. Come on. Let's get that coffee. You might feel differently. You can't keep this up. Sooner or later, we'll have to tell Gwyneth you made it back. Whether you choose to see her or not is your business."

"Mac, I want to be long gone before she finds out. Enough time and she'll have started on a new life. If I'm clear across the country, what choice will she have? I'll simply send divorce papers and she can move on."

"But, Brady—"

He held up his left arm where a hand should be, felt his face burn, and lowered the stump to his side. "Once the holidays are over. I don't want to give her any grief. Not now."

"I met Gwyneth, remember? That woman will love you, divorce papers or not. You aren't giving her much credit." Mac's gaze bore into him, daring him to believe. After all, it was the season of miracles, right?

"Enough! My mind's made up. You said you'd help me find some work until my pension starts. Are you going to or not?" Brady pressed his arm tighter to his body. He still couldn't accept that the rest of it was gone. Maybe once his prosthetic was finished.

"Fine. But I'm telling you. You're making a huge mistake."

"Then it will be my mistake to make. We're friends and you're my boss, Mac, but I won't let you treat me like a child."

Mac made a clicking sound through his teeth and turned his back. "Then stop acting like one."

Chapter Two

"Mommy, can we go today? You promised. Pleeeaase."

Gwyneth couldn't help but notice the way Isabellas's little nose dipped in the front when she said please. How could she deny this precious child anything? Especially now.

"We'll go this afternoon, Izzy. First you have to put your toys away and then get a bath."

"A bath?"

"A bath. Santa won't want a dirty little girl sitting on his lap. Now scoot and take care of your room."

Gwyneth glanced once more at the checkbook. She'd penny-pinched while Brady was gone and had put away a tidy sum for his return. Still, she would have to think about taking a teaching position again. Perhaps if she just subbed, she could earn enough part time until Isabella started school. Then she could teach full time and they would make ends meet well enough.

Without Brady. Without the wonderful husband she had met in high school, dated all through college, and married as soon as they both graduated. He'd gone after the one love in his life: the military. His flat feet had kept him from the service, so he did the next best thing. He went overseas as a civilian consultant. How was it flat feet were good enough for civilian work?

She slapped another tear from her cheek and hollered up the stairs. "Izzy, hurry up with your room."

"Awmost done, Mommy."

Brady cursed under his breath before looking upward. *Sorry, Lord. But I thought I'd dodged uniforms. Will I even be able to do this?*

He pulled the belt tighter with his right hand the best he could and donned his hat. Maybe he should sell burgers. No, they wore uniforms, too. At least it was a job. In a few weeks he'd have his pension. Living on as little as possible and send a direct deposit to their bank account with the rest. Gwyneth couldn't know. Who would have thought a thirty-year old would have to live on a disability pension? There were things he could do, surely. But Mac had said he deserved to take it easy after what happened.

Brady would have to think on that.

With a shudder he pulled on his boots. The left one squeezed the still tender foot. Roadside bomb. How he'd love the opportunity to roadside them. "Ugh." His breath hitched in pain. Well, he couldn't groan on the job. He'd scare everyone half to death. That was Brady. Half dead. No arm, bum leg. Yup. Half a man.

The rotund manager with the bald head poked around the corner. "You about ready, young fella? Gotta get a move on or there'll be plenty of upset folks."

You'd think he was handing out money at Fort Knox instead of…so embarrassing. And folks surely would notice a sleeve tucked into his waistband. Would they think he could do his job without a lot of questions? He rose, putting pressure on his cane.

The man stared at him for a second. "Say, that's a nice touch."

Brady gulped at what he'd like to say. Instead, he just smiled and tried his best not to limp to his work station.

Chapter Three

Gwenyth whispered in her mother's ear. "I have a few pack-ages to pick up without little eyes seeing. If you could take her, what a help that would be."

Her mother patted her hand. "Of course. We'll visit Santa and meet you for lunch." She gazed at Izzy all dressed up in her poofy pink jacket and matching hat and mittens. "How does that sound sweetie?"

Without a word, Isabella waved her hand at her mother and scooted along to the front of the store, pulling Grandma with her.

Gwenyth remembered last year. Brady had tossed Isabella on his shoulder and traipsed to see Santa. He'd laughed loud and bois-terous like an overgrown kid, and she had giggled the whole way. Not once afraid to sit on the jolly old fellow's lap. What would Isabella do this year without her daddy? Maybe she should have gone along.

Instead, Gwyneth sprinted for the back of the store where her packages waited in layaway. She'd rush them to the car and then dash back maybe in time to see Isabella have her picture taken with Santa.

Brady spied Isabella before he recognized his mother-in-law, Dodie. What were they doing on this side of the city? His gaze darted from one place to the other. Trapped. He couldn't very well jump up, run, and hide.

"And then a new wagon," the little boy shouted. "Are you listening to me?" The boy tugged at Brady's empty arm and pinched him where it was still very much alive and tender.

"Hey!"

"Well, you weren't listening. Did you hear me say a new wagon?"

"Ho, ho, ho." Brady made eye contact with the mother who nodded. "A new wagon it will be. Here." He handed the boy a candy cane, though he wanted to dump the little monster on the ground. Probably would get him fired, so he smiled instead. Where had Isabella and Dodie gone?

He saw ten more children before time for a break, then he spotted Isabella. Dodie let go of the mittened hand and an elf lifted his precious little daughter onto his lap.

"Hi, Santa. Golly, you have nice eyes. They're all smiley. You look like—"

Without thinking, Brady wrapped his arm around his daughter and began to sob.

Dodie pushed forward. "What's going on? Izzy, you all right?"

"He's okay, Grandma. He has smiley eyes." Then she glanced again. "Oh, are you sad? Your eyes have tears."

Brady brushed at his face over his beard, still clutching Isabella to him. "I just…"

"See here." Dodie leaned forward. "Are you drunk? Let go of my granddaughter. What's wrong with you?"

And with that, she grabbed Isabella under the arms and swished her out of the store.

"Oh, come now, Mom. Surely you must have—"

"I'm telling you, he started to cry. No, he didn't cry. He sobbed. Like a baby. I think he was drunk. What kind of men do they hire?"

Gwyneth crooked her head toward Isabella and mouthed, little pitchers…

She'd see to Santa Claus. She felt mother tiger, as Brady used to call her, rising up. Maybe he was a pervert. Well, she'd make short order of that creep.

"You and Izzy go for a hot chocolate and Mommy is going to go speak with Santa. *And* the store manager."

"Did Santa do something wrong, Mommy? He had nice eyes."

"No, Mommy just thought she'd thank him for giving you the candy cane."

"But he didn't. We left."

"Then *I'll* get you a piece of candy before I'm done." She turned to Dodie. "And I'll give *him* a piece of my mind."

The sound of her shoes clacked louder than an old-fashioned typewriter as she stormed across the store. How dare he frighten her baby? Brady would have had plenty to say if he was here.

But he wasn't here. He might never be with them. There it was. Waterworks again.

He heard her footsteps before he saw her. In mother tiger mode if he was right. Oh, boy. He set down the last child and asked his elf to put out the Santa's Feeding His Reindeer sign, but not in time.

"Just where do you think you're going, *Santa?*" She grabbed for an arm that wasn't there, and he saw the look of pity in her eyes. Just what he'd thought. She would pity him if he came back. Not gonna happen. "Sorry. But what's the idea of scaring my little girl?"

Brady raised his voice a notch to mask his and hoped it didn't make him sound like an idiot. "I didn't mean to. I was just remembering something. I'm very sorry."

Her face softened. "Well, of course. Things happen. But you're working with children. They upset so easily."

Brady cleared his throat. Had Isabella been frightened? "Izzy didn't look upset." He choked on his words. "Here, give your little girl a candy cane for me." He held out the candy, praying she hadn't heard.

"Izzy? How do you know her name? Are you some kind of stalker or weirdo? How do you know my daughter?" She smashed the candy cane under foot and turned, but only for a moment.

"Santa?" She whirled around, recognition in the mother tiger's blue-blue eyes.

"Gwynnie. I'm sorry, I thought I could stay away."

She stumbled forward. "Why? Why would you want to do that?"

He held up the cane, smacked it against the brace on his leg. Wiggled his shoulder so that the sleeve flopped pathetically.

"Oh, Brady. Do you think I'd care about that? Babe, I just want you home. With Izzy, with me."

Brady pulled her against him and tears flowed into her hair. Mac had been right. Gwyneth *didn't* care. The beard tickled as his lips caught hers. She laughed and so did he, but it didn't stop them from kissing again and again.

Isabella appeared out of the corner of his eye. She started jumping up and down and clapping.

"Grandma, come 'ere. Quick. Santa Claus is kissing Mommy! Can he do that?"

About the Author

Linda is an author and agent for Hartline Literary Agency. Linda writes romance: historic, and suspense. There's nothing she likes better than a sweet kiss interspersed with keeping watch over her shoulder. She's married and has three kids and three grandchildren. She loves theatre almost as much as books. Loves singing, costuming, and just hanging around the theatre in general. She also longs for the moment when a book is done as well as finding that perfect client to represent. All in all, she's just plain happy with a book in her hands, her own, or one from a client.

You can find Linda online at:

http://lindaglaz.blogspot.com/

http://hartlineliteraryagency.blogspot.com/

A Christmas for Maddie

CHRISTINA RICH

Dedicated to Maddie, and to all the families
who have lost a child much too soon.

ISAIAH 61:1-3
The Spirit of the Lord God is upon me;
because the Lord hath anointed me to
preach good tidings unto the meek;
he hath sent me to bind up the brokenhearted,
to proclaim liberty to the captives, and the opening of the prison to them that are bound;
To proclaim the acceptable year of the Lord,
and the day of vengeance of our God;
to comfort all that mourn;
to appoint unto them that mourn in Zion, to give
unto them beauty for ashes, the oil of joy for mourning, the garment of praise for the spirit of heaviness;
that they might be called trees of righteousness, the
planting of the Lord, that he might be glorified.
(King James)

Honeysuckle Valley, KS
1867

"Miss Wilson."

Maddie startled and jumped to her feet, dropping her mother's torn gown. The crimson velvet pooled on the frigid whitewashed planks of her classroom. Although she had hoped Caleb Monroe would come and had tried to prepare her nerves at seeing him for the first time since he'd broken off their engagement, she still pressed her hand against her chest to calm her thundering heart.

However, nothing could have prepared her for the way her knees shuddered or her insides quaked. She'd never seen him with so much as a dusting of a day's shadow coloring his jaw, and now he sported a full beard as if he'd gone months without a razor. Gone was the youthful man who'd courted her. In his place was a man matured by life, hardened by trials. She was a bit nervous, but not in a frightened sort of way. Caleb wouldn't harm her, or anyone else for that matter, but from the thunderous expression, she knew without a doubt to tread with caution.

Drawing in a slow breath, she dropped her hands to her sides and skirted around the desk. Surely the sturdy piece of furniture her father had ordered for her upon her letter of acceptance as the new teacher would be enough to protect her from whatever danger Caleb posed. Perhaps the glossy sheen would be sufficient to deter the fluttering in her chest and remind her that the man hulking just inside the doorway had chosen a very different path for her. "Mr. Monroe."

The door closed behind him, shutting out the gray light of afternoon and fresh air, but not before she'd caught the high color in his cheeks. His anger pulsed between them.

Good!

Perhaps now they could discuss his ward's behavior.

The heel of his boots struck the floorboards as he barreled toward her. Each step threatening to steal her breath. She'd always respected his solid strength and work ethic, but she'd been taken mostly with his compassion for the townsfolk. Caleb Monroe had been a cheerful giver, always there to lend a hand and a comforting word, much like his father, Reverend Monroe.

Caleb had been a constant shoulder after she lost her mother. A help at the mercantile while her father mourned. And then Caleb was gone. It was as if he, too, had perished when the cholera struck their community.

Maddie understood Caleb had needed to care for his sister's family as they struggled against the claws of death. She understood the pain of his loss. At least Caleb had his nephew Thad and his father, just as she had hers. Some in Honeysuckle Valley weren't so fortunate. They were all still trying to pick up the pieces, to find joy and laughter.

All except Caleb.

His disappearance had caused many to believe he'd perished too. But she knew better. Her heart would have dried up and crumbled to pieces like day old bread left for the birds if he had succumbed to the illness. Besides, even if Caleb's nephew didn't care for her much, he would have told her if Caleb has passed on. Most likely not with good intentions, but rather to see her hurt. Thad had gone from a sweet child to one causing all sorts of mischief. Picking fights with the older boys had been expected. The snakes and frogs hidden in desks had been a devilish sort of thing, but today… today was a whole different matter.

Caleb lifted the rim of his hat about to remove it. He obviously thought better of it after waves of hair fell over his eyes. She always pondered how he'd look with his hair a mite longer, and now she wished she'd never thought of such a thing. Especially since her fingers itched to run through his chestnut locks and tuck the wayward strands behind his ear. Disappointment cloaked her shoulders when he shoved his hair back beneath his hat.

He pressed his hands against her desk and leaned forward. The scent of cloves, oranges and freshly cut wood along with leather and horse swirled around her, causing her to inch backwards. After he'd broken their engagement, she'd tossed every clove from the house.

Where Caleb's thick buckskin coat had once hung loose as if he were no more than a ruddy youth, it now stretched tight across his shoulders. She found it odd how several months could change a man's appearance, especially when so many people remained frail.

He cleared his throat. She stared at his eyes. The one place she'd tried to avoid looking since he'd made his presence known. The silver light of his eyes pierced through her, renewing the heartache she'd long since tried to bury. The mischief, the laughter, the love... gone.

"Miss Wilson, whatever is, or was between us is just that, between us."

Maddie knitted her brows together. His deep timbre echoed in the empty schoolhouse and goose pimples rose on her arms. She quite regretted leaving the wood stove unattended after class dismissed, but she hoped her prayers for a Christmas snow would be answered. And she wanted to know the moment the weather shifted from the unusual spring-like temperatures. "Mr. Monroe, you misunderstand."

He raised his calloused hand, cutting off her words. "Punishing my nephew because you're angry with me is unbecoming."

Maddie sucked in a sharp breath. "Mr. Monroe, if you would have answered my first five summons."

His dark brows furrowed beneath the shadow of his hat. He paced back before crossing his arms over his chest. "It does not matter if this is the first time or the sixth time you've *summoned* me. Having Sheriff Trail dump Thad in a cell like a hardened criminal is beyond any childish game we played as youngsters. You will not use my nephew as a pawn to gain my attention. Do I make myself clear?"

Appalled at his allegation, Maddie brought her hand back, ready to strike Caleb's stiff jaw, but she quickly dropped her shaking arm to her side. "Mr. Monroe, I assure you this is not a game and I will not respond to your accusations with violence, no matter how offensive they may be."

Caleb watched as Maddie opened her desk drawer, pulled out something, and tossed it at him. The object slid down his chest and would have landed on the floor next to the velvet gown or the puddle of muddy water dripping from his boots had he not caught it against his coat. A tinge of guilt knotted in his gut at the mess he'd tracked in, but it couldn't be helped.

He pulled his hand from his chest and examined the thick braid the length of his arm, tied with a fancy red ribbon. Shifting his weight, he lifted his gaze to Maddie's dark brown eyes rimmed with tears. He had forgotten what it felt like to be her champion and for a moment he wanted to be that man again. But he wasn't. Those days were gone. She needed a man who could pull her into his arms and tell her all would be right as rain. And no matter how much he longed to be that man, he wasn't, nor could he ever be. He'd seen too much hurt to lie to her. Rain was never right, not even when the ground cracked from too many months of thirst.

"What is this?"

She turned away from him, her blue skirt dancing around her feet as she glided toward the window. "Anna Beth's hair."

Maddie lifted a trembling hand toward her face. A sickening feeling clogged in his throat. He should have been a better comfort to Maddie, but after watching his sister lose her worthless husband, and then standing by as she died of grief after her baby girl passed too, Caleb had known he wouldn't survive losing Maddie. Or any children they might have in the future. So he'd walked away.

"What does Anna Beth's braid have to do with Thad?" Inwardly, he already knew.

Drawing in a breath, Maddie lifted her shoulders and faced him. Strands of honey colored hair sprung from the knot at her nape and curled around the cup of her ear. He didn't need to lean in to smell the lavender emanating from the heat of her skin, it permeated the entire room. It had bathed him the moment he'd crossed the threshold.

Maddie tilted her chin, compassion, or was it pity, filled her eyes. "Thad has not been the same child."

Caleb straightened his spine. "What did you expect after losing both parents?"

"Every child in my classroom has lost someone. A parent, a sibling. Some would have nobody left except Mrs. Cook turned her boardinghouse into a home for those orphaned. And let me tell you, Mr. Monroe, not one of them has behaved as badly as Thad. If you would have come after my first summons then perhaps we could have dealt with his behavior before it came to this." She crossed her arms. "I have tried multiple times to contact you. I even spoke with your father."

Caleb flinched at the mention of his father, but wondered what wise words he had offered Maddie.

She straightened under his gaze. "I had no choice but to contact Sheriff Trail."

He rolled his shoulders and then sagged beneath the truth. He'd failed his nephew. He'd failed her. If he'd swallowed his pride and asked his father for help, maybe Thad would have found the love he needed and Anna Beth would still have her hair. He tucked the braid into his coat pocket. He'd think of something to right this wrong. "My apologies, Miss Wilson."

Caleb turned on his heel and stalked toward the door. He placed his hand on the knob, and then halted. "Maddie, why are you destroying your mother's Christmas dress?"

Silence further chilled the schoolhouse. He glanced over his shoulder to see her swiping tears as she stooped to pick the velvet gown from the floor.

"I fear it is Honeysuckle Valley's only hope for Christmas." She leaned her hip against her desk, the torn gown clutched to her chest as rivulets slid down her pale cheeks.

Caleb ignored the overwhelming urge to run to her and gather her in his arms. Instead, he eased out the door and stood on the top step. What had Maddie meant by their only hope for Christmas? And how did she think a simple dress could rectify the situation?

He removed his hat and lifted his face to a sky thickening once again with dark clouds. They'd gone most of the year without a drop. Until the last month. Rain. Rain. And more rain, until mud seeped into every nook and cranny of his late brother-in-law's place. Caleb had worked his fingers raw to close all the holes in the roof so Thad could sleep without a constant deluge on his forehead. That hadn't stopped the creek bed from overflowing into their home. Fortunately, his brother-in-law had built the barn on a rise, giving them and the livestock a dry place to lay their heads temporarily.

He scrubbed his hand over his face and through his hair. "Well, at least the boy won't have to bed down with the animals tonight."

Caleb clamped his hat back down and paced the floor. He had a mind to get Thad released so he could spank him a good one, but after the way Thad's pa had beat him for the slightest wrong, Caleb didn't dare.

Time to cool his heels before he spoke with the sheriff about his nephew. Since they only had a few weeks' supplies left at the farm, he might as well order what he was going to need now. Only problem was he'd have to face Maddie's pa at the store.

Caleb stomped the mud off his feet outside before opening the door. The mercantile was much warmer than the schoolhouse causing him to wonder if Maddie had run out of wood.

"Good day to you, sir." Mr. Wilson stepped from behind a curtain, wiping his hands on his apron.

"Hello, Mr. Wilson."

The older man's bushy brow sunk down in the middle. "Caleb? Caleb Monroe?"

"Yes, sir."

Mr. Wilson rushed toward him, his hand held out and joy in his eyes. Maddie's pa grabbed hold of his hand then pulled him into a hug. "It's good to see you, son. You've been missed."

Son? Missed?

"Si—ir." Caleb cleared his throat. He stepped back, pulled his hat from his head and held it against his chest like a shield. "I'm in need of a few supplies before heading back to the farm."

Mr. Wilson laughed. "What might you be needing, son?"

Surprised at Mr. Wilson's laughter, Caleb took another step back and glanced around the empty mercantile. How could this man who'd lost his wife to a brutal sickness find anything to laugh about? "Uh, do you have any flour?"

It'd been a while since he'd had griddlecakes.

"Sorry 'bout that, Caleb. The supply wagon hasn't been through in a few weeks. The creek has been too high and the roads too muddy. About the only thing I have left are molasses and that awful fabric the color of tobacco stained teeth. The one Mrs. Cook ordered to make the young 'uns clothes for Christmas. Turns out it's not the *right* color."

Is that what Maddie meant about no Christmas? Caleb brushed his hand over one of the shelves. "Did Mrs. Cook ever get her fabric?"

The corners of Mr. Wilson's mouth turned downward. The light in his grey eyes dimmed. "No. I feel awfully bad about that. I'd go to Leavenworth myself but the creek is too high, and I don't wish to leave Maddie alone so close to Christmas. She wants something terrible to bring joy to the children, but we can't even find a decent tree."

Caleb twisted his lips. "Forgive me for saying so, Mr. Wilson, but I'm surprised anyone would want to celebrate after what happened."

"And why would that be?" A familiar voice broke into their conversation.

Caleb snapped his gaze beyond Mr. Wilson's shoulder and toward the man behind the counter. "Pa?"

"Caleb." His father nodded. "You didn't answer my question. Why do you think we wouldn't want to celebrate the birth of our Savior?"

He pulled air in through his nostrils and swallowed past the thick knot of dust in his throat. "Our Savior? The one who claims to never leave us or forsake us?" Caleb wanted to rant at God for allowing his sister and Maddie's mother to die, for allowing the pestilence to destroy their town.

"We are not destroyed, son. And, yes, he's our Savior."

Caleb's body stiffened, not realizing he'd spoken the words aloud.

"We are rising up because we have hope. Hope that God will turn our ashes into beauty. Yes, we mourn. Scripture tells us there is a time for such, but there is also a time to dance, a time to rebuild. If you open your eyes, you'll see."

Caleb clenched his fingers around the rim of his hat. "What I see are empty shelves."

"Only for a moment, Caleb," Mr. Wilson offered. "Soon, they will be filled to bursting."

Caleb shook his head. "How can you be certain?"

Mr. Wilson laughed. "I have faith in the good Lord, Caleb. We needed the rain to water the thirsty ground so when spring comes it'll be ready to take the seeds."

The bell above the door jangled. Anna Beth, hair chopped and barely hidden under a bonnet, ran into the store carrying a plate of cookies. Guilt filled Caleb's chest as he looked at the poor girl just a few years younger than Thad.

She halted next to him and craned her neck. "Ma saw you come in here. I know Thad is in trouble and all, but I wanted to take him Ma's cookies. They're the best in Honeysuckle Valley."

He knelt in front of her. "Why would you want to do that after what he did to your hair?"

Her mouth widened, revealing a few missing teeth. "Because Miss Maddie said forgiveness is important."

"She did, did she?" He knew the scriptures and knew God would forgive him, but would Maddie forgive him for acting a fool?

"She also says sometimes a boy just needs to know people care."

Caleb glanced at his father. He'd always known his father's love, always would. Even when they disagreed. Even when he'd left home in a fit of anger to care for his sister. Thad hadn't been as fortunate. Unfolding to his full height, Caleb rested his palm on Anna Beth's shoulder. "I think it'd be all right if you and your ma visited Thad."

The little girl rewarded him with a brilliant smile. "Thank you, Mr. Monroe. And don't worry about my hair none. Ma says it was due for a good trimming."

Anna Beth skipped out the door and his heart filled. He turned to Pa and Mr. Wilson. "I'm afraid I owe you both an apology."

His father walked toward him and wrapped his hand around Caleb's neck. "I love you, Caleb."

"I know, Pa." He shifted his feet. "I need to take care of some things, but I'll be back in a few days. I'll see Thad's released from jail when I return. He could use some time to think on what he's done. When I do, would it be all right if we come home? He needs a good man in his life."

His father pulled Caleb close. "Thad has a good man in his life, but two wouldn't hurt."

Caleb swallowed the emotion in his throat and stepped back. "Pa, Mr. Wilson." He jammed his hat onto his head and walked out of the mercantile.

Maddie closed the book and set it on the sheriff's cluttered desk. She rose from her chair and arched her back.

"You think Caleb is going to leave me here to rot?"

Opening the cell door, Maddie sat onto the cot next to him. According to her father, Caleb had left town four days ago, shortly after their confrontation at the schoolhouse. She wished he'd come back. It'd leave his father brokenhearted once again, not to mention Thad. She leaned her head against the limestone wall, pleased to feel its coldness. The temperature outside was finally dropping. Now if only the incessant rain would turn to snow in time for Christmas. She nudged his shoulder with hers. "You don't think you deserve to stay here?"

His gaze dropped to the floor. "Probably. It was a terrible thing I did, cutting off Anna Beth's braid. I can't believe she brought me cookies."

Maddie smiled. Forgiveness was powerful, for both parties involved.

"You think Sheriff Trail will let me out tonight? I can't wait to see the decorations. Pa never let us do any at home."

Maddie didn't want to ruin Thad's excitement, but she sure didn't want him to be disappointed either. "I'm afraid there won't be a tree this year. We couldn't find one worthy of a Honeysuckle Valley Christmas."

They couldn't find one anywhere that wasn't scraggly.

He shrugged his shoulders. "That's all right. You think there'll be cookies?"

"I have it on good report there might be one or two." Maddie winked.

The door flung open, ushering in a burst of cold air. Caleb stood in the doorway, hunkered down in his coat. Thad jumped off the cot and ran out of the cell before throwing himself at his uncle. "I'm sorry for what I did, Caleb. I won't ever do it again. I promise. Please don't leave me."

Caleb maneuvered them inside and shut the door. He wrapped his arms around the boy and kissed the top of his head. He lifted Thad's face to him. "I love you, Thad. I'm here to stay, and so is your grandfather."

At that moment, Reverend Monroe walked through the door. Feeling like an intruder, Maddie's cheeks filled with heat as the family embraced each other. She didn't know whether to stay put or to grab her coat and gloves and vacate the jail.

"Come along, Thad. Sheriff said you could go home." Reverend Monroe wrapped a coat around his grandson and ushered him outside.

Maddie chewed on her bottom lip, waiting for Caleb to follow. He sat in the empty chair beside the sheriff's desk and removed his hat. His chestnut locks curled at various odd angles, begging to be smoothed down. He toyed with the rim of his hat for a few seconds, and then pierced her with his silver eyes. His gaze caught hold of the flickering lamp light. The spark, the love shining had to be an illusion. A Christmas wish never to be. She rose off the cot and stepped from the cell.

Caleb stood. "You look real nice, Maddie."

Heat filled Maddie's cheeks as she brushed her hands over the green calico.

"All Christmas-like." He moved closer. His height and the width of his shoulders crowded the small space, making it difficult for her to breathe. She had to leave, had to go outside, far from his presence before she fainted. He reached for her coat just as she did. The warmth of his touch sizzled a trail up her arm, to her heart, and all the way to her toes. Love for him burned in her chest. But his past rejection sprang to mind. Tears pressed against the back of Maddie's eyes. She darted for the door, her coat could hang. The cold would do her some good.

"Here." His soft timbre halted her every muscle. He moved behind her, holding her coat out.

"Thank you," she said as she reached for the doorknob. Again, Caleb was there. His hand on hers, sending a wave of awareness throughout her entire body. An awareness that no longer belonged.

They stepped onto the plank walkway and strode in silence toward the schoolhouse. Caleb offered his arm as they neared the stairs. Maddie glanced up at him, scared of all the love bubbling within her. She had to remember he no longer cared for her, that he didn't want to marry her.

"A little girl said you told her forgiveness was important. Is that true?"

She blinked. "Yes."

"God and I did a lot of talking over the last few days. I was wrong and I let pride get in the way. I was hurting, but that was no excuse for hurting you. Will you forgive me for acting a fool?"

She smiled and slipped her arm through his as her boot hit the bottom step. "Of course, Mr. Monroe."

Their boots thumped against the stairs. Their breaths puffed into the cold air. They both hesitated at the top, and then Caleb opened the schoolhouse door. Maddie's eyes opened wide as she sucked in a deep breath. The entire town had gathered inside. Cakes and cookies graced the tops of the children's desks that had been pushed to the side. A beautiful green tree stood in the corner, decorated with all the bows she'd made from her mother's dress. Beneath and on the tree was a heap of gifts.

Her father and Rev. Monroe, along with Thad, waved to her from another corner.

"Merry Christmas."

Maddie worried her lip and then she glanced up at Caleb. "You did all this?"

He smiled and her pulse raced like the north wind barreling around the corner of the schoolhouse. "Yes. It's a Christmas gift for you, Maddie."

"I cannot believe... how, how did you do it?"

"I traveled to Leavenworth. Mrs. Cook needed the right color fabric." Caleb winked, and then he grabbed hold of her hands. "Maddie, I know I have no right, but I love you. I've never stopped loving you. I spoke to your father, and if you're willing... well, my pa is willing and I just wondered...." He took off his hat and knelt down on one knee. "Maddie Wilson, will you do me the honor of becoming my bride? Tonight?"

"Tonight?"

He unfolded his length and pressed her against him. "Yes, Maddie, tonight."

The townfolk cheered and clapped.

She closed her eyes to hold back the tears of joy.

"Maddie?"

"Yes." She stretched on the tip of her toes and flung her arms around his neck. "Yes, Caleb Monroe, I will marry you tonight."

He pulled back and met her gaze. "You sure?"

"Yes."

"Good, it's getting a little cold out here." He touched his lips to hers.

"Look, it's snowing!" Anna Beth's voice carried through the haze of love cloaking Maddie. She'd hoped for a Christmas snow, had hoped for a joyous Christmas for Honeysuckle Valley.

Having Caleb return home and declaring his love to her was her best wish come true.

About the Author

When she was younger, Christina Rich tried to dig herself to China, loved *Three Billy Goats Gruff*, and had an obsession with maps. She gave up her dig to China but still jumps at the chance to travel even if it's just down the road. She loves watching modern takes of fairytales and mythologies on the big screen and still has a huge obsession with maps. The older the better.

Born and raised in Kansas, where she currently lives with her husband and children, Christina loves to read stories with happily ever afters, research, take photos, knit scarves, dig into her ancestry, fish, visit the ocean, write stories with happily ever afters and talk about her family and Jesus.

Christina is an author of historical Christian romance set in Ancient Judah and her debut novel, *The Guardian's Promise*, released from Love Inspired March 2014.

You can find more about her at www.threefoldstrand.com

the Littlest Wise Man

K AREN C AMPBELL P ROUGH

"Mom? It's me. Kevin." He gripped the phone receiver in his trembling hand and lowered his voice. "Yes. Something's wrong. She lost the baby . . . our second son. Last night. I didn't want to disturb you." His drawn and tired face registered anguish, as he listened to the voice on the other end of the line.

"Yes, Brian's fine. Our neighbor watched him. I know. It's been rough. Linda's doing fairly well. I left her sleeping and came home to be with Brian. No, that'll be in the doctor's report. Ah, what do you call it . . . still birth?"

In the far corner of the room, a sturdy, three-year-old boy pushed a green tractor across the carpeted floor. He crawled on hands and knees and made his way toward Kevin. "Rrrr! Rrrrr . . . rrr!"

"No, don't think he'd understand, so we're not telling him we lost the baby." His voice broke, and he didn't see Brian pause and look up with open concern on his tiny face. "No, Mom. It won't be much of a Christmas. No . . . with Dad so sick and all you can't fly out here. The church people will help us. I don't think we'll celebrate Christmas . . . just let it go. I know he'll be four next month, but I think he's too young to miss the decorations."

The boy didn't seem to be listening. His chubby fingers explored the intricate parts of the miniature tractor, but his serious blue eyes clouded with concentration.

"Okay. Thanks, Mom. I appreciate it, but we don't need money for the arrangements. Yes. He was so . . . tiny. Oh, Mom, so perfect!" For a moment, Kevin struggled to compose himself. He wiped his cheeks with the back of his hand. "Look, I have to go.

Brian's here with me. I can't . . . say much more. Just pray. I know Dad can't make the trip. We love you. Give Dad a hug."

As he replaced the phone, his son stood up and left the forgotten tractor. "Where's Mommy?" His bottom lip trembled. "I want Mommy."

Kevin knelt on one knee and drew his son close. "She's resting at a big place called a *hospital*. Remember, we showed it to you last week? And when she's rested, she'll be back home with us. Maybe, a couple days? Can you be my big boy and wait for Mommy to get rested?" He tousled the youngster's blond hair.

The child considered the question and nodded. "Is she taking a nap?"

"Yes, and I think we ought to go lay down for awhile. I'm pretty tired. Do you know . . . I was awake all night? Well, I was." He stood up with Brian in his arms, his rough unshaven chin touching the boy's soft childish skin. "Come on, let's take a nap, then I'll call Mommy and let you talk to her. Okay?"

With the utmost care, Kevin rearranged the blankets over the lap of the slender woman on the couch. "Comfortable? Want the lights on the tree turned off? Are they bothering you?"

"No," Linda murmured, a half-smile crossing her tired face. "Did you see his expression, when you plugged in the lights? I wish we had gotten around to putting the tree up . . . before." Her hand moved in a vague motion.

"It was fine this way," Kevin said and sat beside her. "It's Christmas Eve. Won't be much of a Christmas for us . . . but he loved the lights, and we love him. He's so precious! So much more . . . now."

"I know," she whispered and snuggled against him. Her lips rested on his neck. "Go tuck him in, he's waiting. Give him another kiss for me. He's very quiet. You don't suppose he knows or understands? I know he's heard people who dropped by and didn't talk too softly. He looked sad, I thought."

"No, didn't you see him laughing at the bulbs? That red one was his favorite. I thought he'd break it! And that silly smile of his got so *huge* when the lights started to blink!" He rubbed at his face and brushed away a stray tear. "Shoot! When does the crying stop?"

"I don't know," she gasped and pressed the back of his hand to her trembling lips. "Oh, I don't know!"

"He's calling me, and he'll be back down the stairs in no time. I better go to him."

Taking the steps two at a time, he hurried to the small boy's room. "Hey son. Sorry, Mommy and I were talking. Here, jump in bed!" He pulled back the covers.

"Read?" The child stood near the bed in his fuzzy blue pajamas. "Please?"

"Well . . . ." He paused and glanced over his shoulder at the open door and stairs. "Okay, real quick. Which book?"

"This one. It's from Granma."

Grabbing him up, Kevin deposited him in the center of the bed and sat on the edge. "Hmmm . . . The Christmas Story. Okay, here it goes. It was a starlit night, and Mary and Joseph were reaching the last mile of their long journey."

When he finished reading the story, Kevin's eyes were wet with unshed tears. "Wasn't that a good story? Here, let me put this book on your nightstand, and you go to sleep."

With blue eyes bright and large, Brian shook his head. "No, got to tell Mommy!" He swung his short legs sideways and flipped onto his belly, so he could slide off the opposite side of the bed. His stocking-clad toes touched the carpet.

"Brian!" Kevin called, but his son ran out of the room.

"Mommy!"

When Kevin reached the living room, he spied the boy crawling up on the couch and into his mother's arms. "Brian, I said . . . ."

"Mommy, baby's not gone."

"What?" Linda gasped, in alarm, her eyes jerking to meet Kevin's astonished gaze. "What did you tell him?"

"Nothing! I read the book my mother sent. You know . . . ."

"Mommy, you didn't lose our baby. Mary . . . and Jo . . . seph have him. They found him. It's Christmas, Mommy, 'cause they got the baby. Don't cry no more, 'cause it's alright!" His chubby hand patted her cheek.

She gasped back a sob and folded the warm body of her firstborn in her arms. "Oh, Brian, Mommy loves you."

"Now, it's Christmas! Don't worry," he whispered, his lips brushing her cheek. Sighing, he cuddled closer. "Mommy, angels sing 'bout the baby. Daddy read it to me." His eyes grew sleepy. "We know where . . . baby is. Angels are singing." A faint smile traced its way across the unmarred contours of his face.

As the twinkling of tiny Christmas lights sent flashes of colors across the dimly lit room, the couple's grief-stricken eyes met. Quietly, their outstretched hands and fingers touched. The greatest part of the hurt in their eyes seemed to melt away.

"Angels are singing," Linda said. She caressed the top of their son's head. A smile quivered on her lips. "It's Christmas, Kevin. Look at his face. Oh, to sleep like that!"

"Hmmm . . . wise little man, isn't he?"

About the Author

Karen Campbell Prough lives with her husband in sunny Florida. She believes her desire to write is a gift from God. Seven of her short stories have been published in a variety of magazines. One of her books of historical fiction, about life in the mountains of Georgia and the 1800's, will soon be published.

You can find Karen online:

Blog: http://www.karencampbellprough.com

Facebook: https://www.facebook.com/karen.c.prough

Twitter: https://twitter.com/kcampbellprough

A Husband for Christmas

PATTY WYSONG

"Dad, you find me a man and I'll marry him." Cassie Roberts laughed and forked a piece of Thanksgiving turkey. "Otherwise I'm done. I'll be the family *spinster*." Her luck with men was well known in the family. If there was a loser in the crowd, she would find him. Truth be told, she had sworn off men after the last fiasco in July.

The living room clock chimed and Cassie gazed at the over-crowded dinner table where the family had gathered for Thanksgiving—her parents, two older brothers, their wives, all six children, and Nana. All were silent, their eyes wide.

Dear Lord, had she really said that out loud?

Dad cleared his throat. "Well…"

Everyone seemed to lean in, listening to hear what he would say.

They had to know she was joking.

Wasn't she?

Cassie opened her mouth to laugh and say she'd only been joking, but the bite of turkey stopped her. A sip of water helped wash down the food.

Dad's hands linked, arching over his still-brimming plate. He smiled and Cassie wilted back into her chair, relieved. Dad would never interfere in her life like that.

"Okay."

What?

Her hand flew to her mouth to keep from spewing the water. "I was just kidding, Dad."

But even as she said the words relief washed over her.

There was Dad's smile again. The one that always made her feel special. "Were you?"

Pandemonium broke loose across the table. Anything Cassie wanted to say would've been lost. Her brothers and sisters-in-law offered their help, Nana clapped her hands, the nieces and nephews all talked at once, and Mom just smiled a funny little I-know-something-you-don't smile.

What did it mean?

More importantly, what had she just unleashed?

Darren Schmidt squared his shoulders, impervious to the first day of December's chill. Determination pushed him forward. As a kid in high school, he hadn't been able to do the one thing he wanted most to do, but tonight that was going to change. He'd been working toward and praying for this very moment for almost ten years. The fact that Dr. Roberts invited him to their house for supper, on his birthday of all days, had to mean something. There was only one desire Darren had for his birthday—permission to date Cassie Roberts.

True, it was old fashioned, but in high school Darren knew that if he wanted to date Cassie he had to ask her father for permission. But Darren was from the other side of town from the Roberts, the son of a factory worker. Back then, he didn't have the money to take her on dates, but as friends they did everything together. It was an easy excuse to not ask her father for permission to take her out.

Then Jennifer had happened. What a train wreck that had been. She hadn't even liked him: she only wanted his help in Biology so she could pass the class, and have access to his older brother. Something it took him six months to figure out.

And by then, Cassie was gone. He wasn't going to let that happen again.

Last year he and Dr. Roberts met at a medical convention. Some would say it was a chance meeting, but it was God's answer to Darren's prayers. Still, he was surprised by the genuine interest Dr. Roberts showed in him. There was no judging him for how he'd hurt Cassie, just interest in the man he'd become. After months of emailing and telephone calls, Dr. Roberts helped Darren secure a position as an anesthesiologist in the same hospital where he practiced. It was still hard to believe.

Although he'd wanted to immediately pursue Cassie when he arrived at his new job, he hadn't. It might be old-fashioned, but he didn't want to mess this up again. That meant facing an old fear and asking for permission before asking Cassie out.

The voices of his brother and friends mocked him. What if Cassie hated him? What if they no longer got along? What if…

Darren shoved the thoughts away and stopped at the Roberts' front door. Deep in his gut he knew this was what he was supposed to do, even if things didn't work out for him and Cassie. At least then he'd be able to put to rest this idea that she was the perfect woman for him. He'd be able to move on.

Pulling in a deep breath of the December air, Darren rapped on the door.

Dr. Roberts opened the door, smiling. "Darren. Come on in." He pulled Darren into a quick hug.

Mrs. Roberts was next with a hug. "Happy birthday, Darren. It's so good to see you."

She remembered it was his birthday? The doubts that nagged him over the years faded some. The only change he could see in Mrs. Roberts was the softening that age had brought to her face, making her prettier. Cassie still looked a lot like her mother. Darren glanced around the spacious living room. There was no sign of Cassie.

"Mrs. Roberts, thank you for inviting me over. I can't believe you remembered my birthday." Had Dr. Roberts just winked at his wife?

"Well, I remembered it was sometime between Thanksgiving and Christmas and asked Jack if he could check around. Imagine my surprise. Isn't that so like God to work out the details? I hope we didn't interrupt any plans you had."

Darren smiled. It was definitely like God. "Between work and settling in here, I haven't had much spare time, so no, I didn't have any plans."

Family pictures lined the mantle, drawing his gaze. The ones of Cassie captured his attention. Mrs. Roberts filled him in on the their sons' families but said very little about Cassie. At supper, she kept filling his plate as she plied him with questions about his life since high school. She seemed pleased with his answers.

Finally he held his hands over his plate. "Thank you, but no more. I haven't eaten this well, or this much, since Easter with Mom and Dad. I can't take another bite."

Dr. Roberts chuckled as Mrs. Roberts rose and carried their dinner plates into the kitchen. "I bet you can when you see what's for dessert."

Thank goodness he had remembered Mrs. Roberts' penchant for dessert and had saved a little room: otherwise he'd be too sick to enjoy it. The lady was a wonderful cook and hostess.

She returned carrying a covered platter. Dr. Roberts cleared a spot for it in front of Darren, who immediately regretted that last helping of dinner.

Mrs. Roberts lifted the cover and smiled. "Happy birthday."

Cupcakes. Chocolate frosted cupcakes complete with sprinkles.

Someone remembered those were his favorites.

Certainty filled him. All the better to have a chance with their daughter.

December first. Darren's birthday. Would she ever forget him? Would she ever quit measuring every man she met against him? It wasn't like he was perfect. Halfway through their senior year of high school he'd tossed out their friendship so he could date another girl—a girl who was too jealous to accept they were only friends.

Two weeks before Christmas, ten years ago, Cassie had dropped off some things at Darren's house. He'd been in the basement, carving, and although he quickly set it behind him, she'd seen the dark box. There were daisies on the lid. Hope had filled her—daisies were her favorites. But only days later he called and told her they couldn't hang out together anymore, and then Cassie knew the carved box was for his girlfriend, not her.

When Cassie's father was transferred yet again, she was relieved to move with them, choosing a junior college near her parents' new home. It had been a good decision, one that launched her into a career she loved. If only her choice in men was as good.

Anticipation tingled through her as she parked her Camry. Nothing like an evening of Christmas shopping to drive away the nostalgia that always visited her on Darren's birthday. Tonight she and Mom were taking Nana Christmas shopping. She dropped the car keys into her pocket and checked her list for the third time since leaving work. Maybe she'd be able to find the perfect gift for Megan.

But all her niece wanted was a younger brother or sister, and since that wasn't going to happen, she had latched onto the idea of a younger cousin. The just-turned-six-year-old was relentless.

Aunt Cassie, I'll just die if I have to be the youngest forever.

Aunt Cassie, it'd be so fun if I had a real baby to rock.

Aunt Cassie, it's been too long since we've had a baby in this family.

Obviously, Megan had overheard someone talking, and Cassie was willing to bet it was either Megan's great-grandmother, Nana, or her grandmother, Gram, Cassie's mother.

The real kicker, though, was on Thanksgiving when Megan had presented Cassie with her Christmas wish list.

Dear Santa,

All I want for Christmas is a baby cousin. I've been a very good girl all year.

Love,

Megan Cassandra Roberts

Someone must've written it down so she could copy it, because there wasn't a single misspelled word.

And since when did Megan send Santa wish lists? None of Cassie's six nieces and nephews had ever done such a thing.

Precocious didn't come close to describing Megan.

If only it were as simple as Megan thought.

Cassie entered the hallway leading to her grandmother's apartment and shook her head. "Nana, you really shouldn't leave your door open like this. You never know what kind of creep might happen along." She closed the door behind her and left her shoes beside her grandmother's sparkly red flats.

The scent of supper cooking drew her into the kitchen. Nana stood at the stove, her Christmas-shopping finery covered by a pressed apron sporting ruffles and poinsettias.

"Hello, dear. You worry entirely too much. Everyone in this building is just as old as I am."

"And that's just the problem. Everyone else in the area knows it, too, and that makes you an easy target." Cassie peered over Nana's shoulder. Cheese sauce. She dipped a finger into the sauce and took a quick step back, avoiding the expected rap to her knuckles. Spicy cheese sauce. Her favorite. What was going on?

Nana raised a sculpted eyebrow. "Your parents had a dinner guest at the last minute. Your mom sent her apologies for having to reschedule our shopping trip and dropped those off." Nana's wooden spoon pointed to a covered platter sitting on the table.

Cassie lifted the cover and smiled. Chocolate frosted cupcakes with sprinkles. Darren's favorites. But how did Mom know that, even after all this time, Cassie celebrated Darren's birthday with cupcakes? She'd been careful to keep that to herself, hadn't she?

Cassie replaced the cover and scowled at it, but Nana's shrewd eyes hadn't missed a thing. Hopefully she didn't know why Mom brought them.

"Have you ever looked for him?"

So much for wishful thinking. As her best friend through high school, Darren had always been welcomed at their home and family get-togethers, so Nana had met him many times.

"No, and I won't." Discussing Darren wasn't something she wanted to do.

"He was the nicest young man, you know. You should've fought for him."

"We were just friends, Nana."

"The best marriages are based on friendships." Using red and green plaid potholders that one of Cassie's nieces made for Nana last year, Nana drew a mini meatloaf from the oven and set it on a familiar wooden trivet. Cassie loved how Nana surrounded herself with family even though she lived alone.

"Asking your father to find a husband for you was one of the smartest decisions you've made yet."

Surely Dad wouldn't do something so…primitive. Cassie made a face, determined not to let Nana draw her into this conversation.

"Set the table, dear, and use the Christmas china. Cupcakes and Christmas china. Fitting, don't you think?"

"Of course. Cupcakes look good on any dish." *If only I could have a real cupcake for Christmas.* Cassie sighed. She refused to chase after Darren like some love-starved school girl.

The bed shook again and Cassie smiled. She opened an eye just a sliver to sneak a peak at the time. Three minutes since the last tremor and two minutes to go before the clock read six—the time Megan knew she could get up, and not a minute before.

Not that Cassie was sleeping, but her niece didn't need to know that. It would be hard enough keeping her under-wraps until 6:30 without adding more time to the ordeal.

Ah, the magic of Christmas morning. It never got old. She started to snuggle into the covers to savor it more but caught herself in time. Any movement at this point would alert Megan she was awake. Part of the fun of Christmas was the sleepover at Mom and Dad's house. They all piled in and stayed up late after the Christmas Eve service. Christmas morning, everyone got up as late as the youngest child could endure. Cassie was no better than the children. That was why she always got the early birds in her room. She grumbled, but secretly she loved it.

All except for the part that she was Aunt Cassie with no uncle snuggled next to her.

Maybe Dad would find her a husband. But did she really want that? Where was the romance? She sighed. Other times she'd had romance and the hurt to go with it. If Dad ever suggested a man for her, she'd seriously consider it—not that she'd ever admit that to anyone.

Ever.

But the thought of being the one modern girl who needed her father to find a husband for her was awful. At the same time, the thought of being alone the rest of her life was worse.

The bed rocketed to life and a small body pounced on her amid a flurry of stuffed animals and blankets. "Merry Christmas, Aunt Cassie!"

Cassie laughed and untangled her arms from the blankets so she could hug Megan. "Merry Christmas, sweetie. Is it 6 o'clock already?"

The blonde bed-head nodded vigorously, clearly proud of herself. The clock read 6:01 and Cassie was impressed. Two minutes later than last year and a new record for the ones sleeping in this room. The other kids popped out of their sleeping bags, grinning and jabbering. Not that it mattered. After all, it was Christmas morning.

All eyes watched the alarm clock on the bedside table. Excitement brewed and bubbled, just like the coffee Cassie could smell as she manned the door, preventing escapes. Finally, the red numbers said 6:30 and she pulled the door open. "Go get 'em, guys."

Dashing straight to the living room, she plugged in the Christmas tree lights and savored the last moment of quiet. The Nativity scene on the mantle drew her attention. *Thank You, Jesus. You've given me so much. Help me to always be thankful for it. No matter if this is all I ever have.*

Eight Christmas coffee mugs were set out, ready for the special brew that dripped into the pot. Eight? Strange. Maybe one of the kids was allowed to drink coffee now—stranger yet.

Soon everyone gathered in the living room, coffee in hand. They settled around the tree. Bulging stockings were propped against the gifts that spilled out from under the lower limbs.

Mom looked at the clock on the mantle, then at Dad. She seemed a little panicked.

"What's wrong, Mom? Did you forget a gift? I'll go get it for you." Cassie set aside her coffee and rose, ready to fetch whatever it was.

"Um, yeah." Mom was acting funny. "Yes! Go in my bedroom, under the bed on my side and see if I forgot a little box wrapped in…in green paper. I can't remember if I brought it out."

Dad winked. "Megan, go with her and help."

Definitely unusual.

Those two had been doing strange things all month, but then again maybe there was something near the tree they needed to hide from Megan.

Cassie lifted the bed skirt. "Crawl under and make sure Gram didn't forget anything." She had been under the bed herself just yesterday, pulling out all the gifts, and she'd swear nothing was forgotten.

Snickers and shushes sounded from the living room, followed by silence then a burst of laughter. Megan shimmied out from under the bed.

"Nothing?"

Megan blew a flyaway piece of hair off her nose. "Not even a dirty sock."

Just as Cassie suspected, there was no forgotten gift.

Together they reentered the living room. No one looked their way. In fact, everyone was busy being sure they didn't look. What a weird family she had.

Christmas stockings were passed out and the chaos descended. It was the only time they'd all open gifts at the same time, and it was a moment of abandoned fun as they opened the little treasures stuffed in their stocking—the latest color of nail polish, pens, lipstick, lotion, a favorite candy she rarely bought for herself.

Soon the floor was littered with small scraps of colorful paper and while the kids played with tiny toys that had been tucked in their stockings, the adults chatted, sipping their coffee and playing with their own version of toys. Her brothers still tried to play it cool but she saw them fiddling with their gifts, especially the telescoping magnet thingie she and Mom had found. She glanced at Mom, but she was busy looking out the window.

Mom's gaze darted back to the clock. "Time for breakfast."

Since when was Mom worried about following the clock on Christmas Day? Whatever the reason, Cassie knew better than to ask about it now. Her nephews had already said they were hungry, many times, and Nana had fidgeted with the place settings while others poured coffee.

Darren parked his car at the curb five minutes before the appointed time and studied the gifts on the seat next to him, praying he'd remembered everyone. It had been hard shopping for people he hadn't been with in ten years, but he'd listened as Dr. and Mrs. Roberts spoke about the family. And the extra two boxes of candy just in case would do nicely.

After his birthday he'd spent time with Cassie's parents every week and his respect for them had grown greater. He hoped to one day be a father like Dr. Roberts. Darren adjusted the gift at the top of the bag closest to him. Cassie's gift, one he'd kept for ten years. Would she recognize it?

He wiped his hands on the legs of his dark brown cords. Had he dressed up too much? Not enough? The roll and coffee he'd downed at his apartment churned, agitated by the waiting and all the unknowns. Half a block away, he saw a candelabra of electric lights being placed in the Roberts' window. The signal for him to come. Darren slumped over the steering wheel. *Your will be done, Lord. You know I've loved Cassie all these years. Please give her a special love for me too.*

The sting of the freezing air gave him an excuse for the way the packages shook in his hands. Clearing his throat, he knocked on the door.

Cassie sat on the floor with Megan in her lap. The little girl was unwrapping a gift from her grandparents and Cassie could feel her excitement. Looking up to smile at Mom, Cassie was distracted by someone approaching the house. Who would interrupt on Christmas morning?

The knock on the door silenced everyone.

Dad smiled. That same special smile he'd given her at Thanksgiving.

Oh no.

What had he done?

She had been kidding.

What was she going to do now?

The room grew fuzzy and sounds blurred. Her mother and grandmother greeted the man with a hug, her brothers jumped from their seats and welcomed him like a long lost brother, and Megan bounced on her lap. Must be a friend of her parents.

Someone pulled Megan away and the unwelcome guest crouched in front of her. His chocolate brown eyes smiled but lines of worry crossed his forehead.

Just as they often had years ago.

Darren.

He held a gift out to her. "Merry Christmas, Cassie."

Cassie's fingers pressed against her lips, willing them to be still. Was he really here? How had Dad found him?

She accepted the gift while her mind grappled with the man in front of her. He was real and cuter than ever.

Darren smiled and Cassie's heart danced. She looked at her father, who stood with his arm around her mother. Dad nodded and a tear ran down Mom's face.

Opening her mouth she tried to speak. "Wh—?" A flush warmed her vocal chords enough that they worked on her second try. "Hi, Darren."

Nana sank back into her chair. "It's Christmas and all you say is 'hi'?" She leaned forward to whisper in Cassie's ear. "Wish him a merry Christmas, child."

Darren winked at Nana and Cassie laughed.

"Merry Christmas, Darren."

"Open your present, Aunt Cassie!" Megan wiggled away from whoever had been holding her back and she knelt beside Cassie.

Darren nodded, encouraging her, so Cassie picked at the bow, then carefully peeled the paper from the cardboard. Folding back the box flaps, she saw the daisy covered walnut box she had caught Darren carving that December ten years ago. With trembling fingers she lifted it out of its nest and met Darren's gaze.

"It was for you, Cassie. But when I finally figured it out that June, you and your family were gone. I'm so sorry."

Cassie rose to her knees and threw an arm around his neck. "Thank you. I hoped it was for me but then…all that other stuff happened. I can't believe you kept it."

His chuckle vibrated as he held her close. "I couldn't let go of it. It was always for you."

Beside them Megan was clapping and jumping up and down. "Aunt Cassie got a husband for Christmas!"

Chaos erupted around them as her brothers and their wives interjected things like "no, it's just a jewelry box he made a long time ago" and "maybe" and "we'll see" and "give them time" but Cassie didn't care. Darren was here. With her. That was enough for the moment.

Who was she kidding? It was enough for a lifetime.

Over Darren's shoulder Cassie spied her parents again. "Thank you."

All of their secretiveness this month finally made sense. They had been with Darren and he was their choice as well as hers. She knew this was just a beginning, that they had plenty of time to get to know each other all over again. This time, she didn't fear the outcome. Her dad was a wise man who loved her. He would never encourage a man who wasn't right for her.

Yes indeed, she had received the best Christmas present ever.

About the Author

Since Patty Wysong quit running from God's call on her life and surrendered her pen to Him, she's been happy. Life is never dull as she juggles being a wife, mom to a handful of kids and a couple of Capuchin monkeys, life on the road, and being a writer. As long as she's obeying God's leading, she figures that sanity is a novelty and not a necessity in the zoo she lives in.

Patty is passionate about encouraging and enabling others to fulfill what God has called them to, and often writes and speaks on those topics. She clings to the promise that God will enable her to do what He asks of her, otherwise she would be living with the scaredy cats at the Funny Farm and not just occasionally visiting.

She would love to connect with you online. You can find her on her blog: http://www.pattywysong.com

Facebook: https://www.facebook.com/patty.wysong

Twitter: https://twitter.com/PattyWysong

Instagram: http://instagram.com/pattywysong/

Pinterest: http://pinterest.com/pattywysong/

A Pinch of Love

Party of the Job

and

With Her Own Eyes

JOANNE SHER

Pinch of Love

Was she ever tired. After a full day of watching six toddlers, Ashley was about ready to collapse.

If the weather had been nicer, it likely would have been a less exhausting, hectic day. Around noon, however, a huge snowstorm blew in, with harsh winds. This had been a day where everyone had to stay in the house – and two-year-olds definitely got restless. It was all she could do to keep them from literally climbing the walls. Fortunately, the storm had cleared, and their parents had been able to get through to pick them up.

Ashley sighed. Unfortunately, her day wasn't over yet. The whole family was coming over tomorrow evening for Christmas Eve dinner, and she had preparations to make. Cleaning, cooking, wrapping gifts – the list seemed endless. Preparing her house for fourteen visitors was not her idea of fun.

"Whatever possessed me to offer to host Christmas Eve?" she grumbled aloud.

Picking up the toys and putting them back in their bins, Ashley wished her mom was still around. She had always hosted this celebration, but with her mom's untimely death last June, it seemed it was now her responsibility. None of her siblings had homes big enough to hold everyone, so she had offered hers.

"I need to at least get into the Christmas mood."

Ashley went over to her stereo and found a station with Christmas music, turning it up so she could hear it throughout the house.

She went into her bedroom and grabbed the presents she needed to wrap. They were modest, as it had been a tough year. Listening to the music, however, she smiled, singing along to her all-time favorite carol, "The Little Drummer Boy."

These gifts, she thought, came from her heart, regardless of how much she spent on them. Baby Jesus received precious, expensive, valuable gifts, but He smiled at a song, which cost nothing.

Finishing up her wrapping, she headed for the kitchen. The rest of the family was bringing much of the food. Her only responsibility was the pies. As she worked, she sighed.

"I'm so tired of baking. I just did it for a party, and now here I go again!"

Begrudgingly, she worked on the pie filling as the oven preheated. Glancing over at the pecan pie recipe, she saw a note her mother had scribbled on the side.

Don't forget to glaze the pecans and to toss in a pinch of love.

She laughed. Only her mother would write something like that. When she'd made the pie last year, mom had come over and whispered to her the "error" in her pie-making ways. Ashley had been pretty grumpy, wallowing in self-pity when she found out the difference not glazing the pecans had made. Mom must have dug out the recipe at some point when she was visiting and scribbled the note.

Mom was definitely not a writer. Ashley had precious few examples of her handwriting. This recipe, she decided, would be treasured. This could have been the last thing her mother had ever written. It was certainly the most precious to Ashley.

As she put the pie into the oven – pecans glazed and a pinch of love added – preparations seemed somehow less daunting. Mother was definitely here helping her along, and she could tell it was going to be a merry, blessed Christmas.

Part of the Job

"Okay, folks. Find your positions," she ordered. "Have you all had your potty break? No delaying the process with halts in production."

My mother had that drill sergeant look about her, so I knew it was time for business. I took my traditional spot at the end of the assembly line and waited for instructions.

Timmy, my younger brother, was flitting back and forth, so I took his hand and reminded him of his spot. He shuffled into place between Dad and me. Beside him was Rebecca, with Mom's spot at the end.

"This shouldn't take very long, guys." Mom put her favorite Christmas CD in the boom box. "With all of us working together, these hundred cards should be addressed, stuffed, stamped, and sealed in an hour. A quick job."

Dad and Rebecca groaned. Mom gave them the evil eye, which almost sent Dad into convulsions.

"Let's review our roles." We all fixed our eyes, albeit reluctantly, on the woman of the house so she didn't feel the need to repeat what we'd heard many times before.

"I'm in charge of the envelopes." She waved them above her head. "I will place the return address and the preprinted mailing address on each one in the proper place, and pass it on to Rebecca."

Rebecca nodded. "And I sign, fold, and stuff our Christmas letter in the envelope, then pass it to Dad. Right?"

"Exactly." Mom smiled at my younger sister. "Just be sure you fold it in fourths, so it will fit nicely in the envelope. And then your father will slide the Christmas card into the envelope."

Dad's eyes twinkled as he saluted. "Yes, ma'am. Open end first."

Mom giggled despite herself and nodded.

"And then I get to put the stamp on. Right, Mom?" Timmy actually sounded enthused about it, unlike the rest of us. Besides Mom, anyway.

I rubbed my little brother's back. "Yup. Then you pass the card to me and I pull aside the ones that need an extra note and seal the others."

"That's right." She looked over her troops. "Are we ready to get started?"

Nods traveled across the production line. Mom stepped into place.

"Okay then. Here we go."

It was actually pretty smooth going to start. I had to remind Timmy exactly where the stamp went, but he got into a pattern quickly after that. We didn't really chatter much while we worked. We'd tried that last year, but the lady in charge hadn't thought much of it.

But then, when we were about halfway through, the unspeakable happened.

The doorbell rang.

Now, first of all, you need to know that nobody *ever* comes to our house without calling first. It couldn't possibly be a door-to-door salesman, as we live in the middle of the country and our front door is almost half a mile from the road. Friends and family always, *always* let us know they're coming.

Timmy screwed up his face. "What was that sound?" (*I told you the doorbell doesn't ring much.*)

Everyone stopped working and stared back and forth from person to person, mouths agape. Dad turned his body and began to leave his post, but Mom put her hand out.

"Don't answer it. We're almost done." She had that glare about her again.

"Are you serious, Mom?" Rebecca's tween attitude was quite blatant.

My mother nodded. "Let's finish up."

We all sighed and got back to work, despite the doorbell ringing three more times. Mom, of course, gave us that same look after each ring.

According to Mom's stopwatch, we completed the task in one hour, twelve minutes and thirty-seven seconds, including our little interruption. Mom was thrilled. We were relieved.

"Now, aren't you glad we didn't allow that doorbell to distract us?" Mom poured a round of hot chocolate. "Who knows how long we would have been delayed? I'm sure, if it was important, they'll come back."

"Maybe we should go back," the blonde mumbled, biting her lip.

The gentleman sighed. "You know that's against the rules. If they don't come to the door, we draw another name."

"I know. It's just such a shame for that family, Mr. McMahon."

"It's part of the job, dear — just part of the job."

With Her Own Eyes

Anna opened the door of her modest hovel and breathed in the scents of the nearby marketplace. It was early by most standards – the peddlers were just setting up shop – but she had important business to attend to.

Ambling down her street, she smiled, knowing what she would see along the way. She had made this walk every day, several times a day, for decades. Certainly, she was moving along slower than she did back when she was young, but the view was the same. At least it was a short distance.

Reaching into her pocket, she pulled out a scrap of bread. A scruffy dog trotted to her, then waited for the old woman to lower her hand. Anna obliged him and patted him on the head with her other hand.

"Good morning to you, too. And that it will be, my canine friend."

The mutt rubbed its furry body against her leg. She chuckled.

"I'm sorry, little fellow, but I have important business. No time to play. The Lord has given me wonderful news, and I must see about it."

This was the event she and her people had been anticipating for centuries. Up until recently, she assumed that it would happen after she was already in Abraham's bosom, an event which, at her age, she suspected would occur soon. But just a few moons ago, the Lord sent her a very special message.

It wasn't the first message she had received from Him. She was a prophetess, after all. But it was certainly the most exciting, the most life-changing.

My dear child, my faithful one, before this year is over, you will see, with your own eyes, my salvation.

Dear Anna, even now He who Isaiah spoke of is growing in the womb of one of my precious children. She will bring Him to the temple after her days of impurity are completed, and I will give you the privilege and responsibility to bless and prophesy about Him in His very presence.

You have been faithful to Me these eighty-four years of your life, Anna, and I will be faithful to fulfill this promise to you, and my people, before I bring you home to be with Me.

The hope in her heart sparked that day and had grown bigger each day since. Her prayers had become more fervent, her trips to the temple more frequent, over the past several months.

"So the Lord says, be ready and repent," she had proclaimed at least daily in the temple courts. "The Messiah – the Christ – is at hand."

"I will see the Lord's Anointed with my own feeble eyes," she'd announced to her reflection daily since the Lord had spoken of it. And this morning, she heard a response.

It will be today, dear Anna. Today, at the time of the morning sacrifice, my Salvation, my Light to the Gentiles, will appear in the temple courts, and to you. Go now, Anna, and see my Anointed One.

"Yes, dear dog, it will be a good day, for today the Lord will show me His salvation."

It was with quickened, yet faltering steps that she entered the temple courtyard moments later. She stopped by the entrance to the temple itself and knelt, reciting her morning prayers. After several minutes, she rose and looked up at the majesty of the temple.

The familiar voice of her dear friend Simeon, a fellow devotee of the Lord, met her ears. Turning toward him, she saw a young couple beside him and an infant in his arms.

She cupped her ear as she approached.

"This child is set for the fall and rising again of many in Israel; and for a sign which shall be spoken against, that the thoughts of many hearts may be revealed." Simeon's gravelly voice lowered, and he turned toward the young woman. "Yea, a sword shall pierce through thy own soul also." ★

Anna's heart leapt in her chest, and she took a few hesitant steps. Soon she stood right beside her friend. Tears running down her cheeks, she gazed into the eyes of the Anointed One resting in Simeon's arms.

"Thank You, Lord."

And there was one Anna, a prophetess, the daughter of Phanuel, of the tribe of Aser: she was of a great age, and had lived with an husband seven years from her virginity; And she was a widow of about fourscore and four years, which departed not from the temple, but served God with fastings and prayers night and day. And she coming in that instant gave thanks likewise unto the Lord, and spake of him to all them that looked for redemption in Jerusalem. Luke 2:36-38.

★ Luke 2:34-35 KJV

About the Author

Joanne Sher is a Jew by birth, a Christian by rebirth, and a children's writer by gift. A native Southern Californian, she now lives happily in West Michigan with her husband and two school-aged children. In addition to writing, she is also a freelance editor, the blogger at the FaithWriters blog, and posts monthly at Jewels of Encouragement, The Barn Door, and Internet Cafe Devotions. Visit her at www.joannesher.com.

Blog: www.joannesher.com
FB: https://www.facebook.com/joannesherwriter
Twitter: https://twitter.com/joannesher

I Hate Christmas

ANNE GARBOCZI EVANS

aquel ripped open the wrapper to one more no-sugar, no-fat, tastes-like-cardboard Skinny Lou's candy bar and stared glumly at the crackling fire. Mumford and Son's *Hopeless Wanderer* played in the background.

Two days until Christmas. She hated the holiday. The overpriced greenery, present giving pressure, waist-fattening carbs: there really wasn't an upside to the season. Girls get their hopes up for the most joyous time of the year, and instead their fiancé dumps them.

Dipping a paintbrush into turquoise oil paint, she made one rough stroke across the canvas intended for cousin Jill. Four years ago on Christmas, Raquel had been engaged and eagerly waiting her fiancé's homecoming from Special Forces training.

Well, the story actually started four years before that. . .

Eight years ago: tenth grade, end of school on a Friday afternoon. The summer sun faded into the horizon as the last class of the day let out. Boots crunched on snow as high schoolers piled towards the buses.

Raquel held her knee-length plaid skirt down against her leggings as the wind tore at her scarf. The school Christmas dance was tomorrow and no one had asked her. She snuck a glance to her left.

There he stood—Sam. His leather jacket covered muscles that did the football team proud. He kicked the stand to his motorcycle and swung up. Rust covered the hub cabs and mud splattered up over the seat. He'd built the bike himself from old parts in his dad's mechanic shop.

She'd been in love with him since elementary school, when she gave Hershey kisses to the entire class as an excuse to give a valentine to him.

A tall blonde girl with nails redder than her lips sidled up to Sam.

Raquel turned away. She hated Christmas.

"Want to go out sometime? Get an ice cream cone?" The words ended in a high-pitched squeak.

She turned to see Chris standing behind her. Chris had skipped two years in school because of being crazy smart. So, despite being a senior this year, his voice hadn't properly dropped yet. His thick glasses steamed over in the cold. Gangly ankles peeked out from jeans that didn't reach all the way down to his white sneakers.

Ice cream? Her fingers would freeze off if the bus didn't hurry and pull into the load zone.

"What I really need is a date to the Christmas dance." She frowned as she said it. Going with Chris would be better than going alone, but barely.

"I'd love to take you." His voice was too eager. And too squeaky.

Seriously, the kid was 16. Wasn't it about time for his voice to drop and his arms to stop resembling toothpicks? She slid up one hand to tug at her hat.

The wind caught her school papers and tore them out from under her arm.

Chris went galloping off after them, over-long legs bobbing up and down in the snow. He was a gentleman. She'd say that for him.

A horn honked right beside her. Raquel jumped, only to see Sam grinning. His clodhoppers pressed into the snow as he sat astride the motorcycle.

"Want to go to the dance with me tomorrow?" His voice was deep, matching those brawny hands of his that gripped the handlebars.

"I, uh, yes." Her voice was a croak.

Snow kicked up on her calves. "Think I got them all." Breathless, Chris bumbled forward, white sneakers raising snow. He pressed the papers into her hands.

Taking off his glasses, he wiped them on the tattered cuff of his gray sweatshirt. Most of the sweatshirt's plastic appliqué of an elephant had peeled off.

He balanced his glasses back on his nose. "Do you want to meet at the dance or—"

"Sam just asked me."

"Oh," Chris blinked. "But you asked me before that." He looked like a devastated puppy dog.

"I'm sorry, Chris. I'm going with Sam now." She kept her gaze averted

"Pick you up at seven then, Raquel." Sam raised his hand for a high five. His chapped calluses brushed across her bare skin. Her heart tumbled over itself.

That's how it had started. A magical dance, a relationship, and then on the Christmas Eve of their senior year, a marriage proposal. Wedding planning dragged out from months to years when he joined the Marines after graduation and applied for special forces. And then that fateful Christmas Eve two years past graduation, after hundreds of letters, mostly hers, he'd shown up in his camo fatigues.

Holly and a sprig of mistletoe decorated the doorway she'd run under. She'd jumped into his arms.

And Sam had said, "I think I'm called to singleness. I'm shipping out tonight to an undisclosed location. Goodbye."

Called to singleness! What did that even mean? He probably had a gorgeous, blonde wife and three babies by now.

Raquel's paintbrush dug into the parchment, dragging a palm frond into the speckled tan of sand.

"Raquel! Help me," five-year-old Benny screeched from the apartment's kitchen.

Her sister had told her to supervise Benny's peanut butter sandwich making. But she had faith in the child.

A knock sounded on the front door.

Her cell started to vibrate. Throwing down the paintbrush, she hit the answer button. "Hello."

"Hey, it's Chris," the voice crackled with static. "I just got back in town. Want to meet up for dinner tomorrow?"

That's right, Chris had been gone someplace. New Mexico? He talked about the heat a lot. He'd been emailing her for the last four years. She didn't really read his emails, though she did reply and vent about her life regularly.

He was working in a hospital these days. An orderly maybe? She'd read a line about a needle shipment being delayed.

"What do you say?" Chris's voice was just barely audible above the static.

"Aunt Raquel," Benny screamed again.

"Uh." Holding onto the cell, Raquel walked to the kitchen. Benny stood on a chair holding the peanut butter jar upside down. Directly underneath it, on the newly-scrubbed countertop, was a quivering blob of peanut butter. At least it wasn't touching her tissue wrapped presents. She'd crafted an oil painting for each family member this year.

Wait, what was that white stuff on the counter?

"I like milk with my peanut butter." Benny's mouth turned up—in an ogre-like smile!

Milk was all over the presents, tissue paper dissolving into a sodden mess. And the oil paint canvases she'd spent six months working on—

The knock on the door became more insistent. The doorbell rang.

Sweeping up the paintings, she hurried to the door. Cell phone still in the other hand, she used her knee and the back of her wrist to twist the door handle.

A five foot ten, bulky-as-they-come man with just a shade of stubble on his upper lip stood in front of her.

"Sam?" Raquel stared.

Sam had a cast on his left leg, a hulking cast with tattoos on it. Even though it must be fifty degrees outside, he wore a sleeveless shirt that revealed his biceps. A U.S. Marine Corps tattoo now decorated his left arm.

She inhaled, hoping it would calm her pounding heart. He didn't want her.

"You were right. I'm not called to singleness." His manly voice carried across the crisp air.

Raquel opened and closed her mouth.

"Tore this tendon five weeks ago in training. The docs say I'll be fine, but the Special Forces isn't taking that chance."

"You're out?" Her gaze ran over Sam's face again.

"As of next week. Honorable discharge papers." His mouth angled downwards in a frown that revealed those perfect teeth of his.

"Oh." She swallowed hard.

"Want to grab coffee tomorrow? That tea leaf place we used to go as kids."

"Do I want to?" She willed herself not to yell. It was scarcely ladylike to show this much enthusiasm.

"Ten a.m.," he said and he was gone. Dramatic entrances, dramatic exits: this was the Sam she remembered.

That's when she heard a little click from the phone in her limp hand. She'd only just hung up.

Oh well, easier than telling Chris "no" to his face. Even in fifth grade, when she'd refused to let him buy her an ice cream sandwich from that truck that drove by the school, she'd felt horrible. He was just intensely pitiable with that oversized head and big glasses.

Maybe she could set him up on a blind date. She had a few bookish friends.

Evergreen wreaths draped the front of the Tea Leaf and the candy shop next door smelled of gingerbread. Little bells tinkled as Raquel entered the coffee shop and the ornamental reindeer out front started singing *Jingle Bells*.

Hand on the button of her red coat, she paused. Was her shirt too revealing? Maybe she shouldn't have chosen the silk v-neck at Macy's last night. Or what if her wool skirt had ridden up in the back? She probably should have just worn jeans. But she wanted him to know she was still interested . . .

"Have a seat already." Sam's eyes laughed as he called for her from across the room.

He'd arrived early too. Sam kicked the chair out for her and she slid in.

Sam's hand had just closed over his Styrofoam cup, dwarfing the thing, when a stranger walked up to their table.

He wasn't handsome exactly, but well-built and tall. His sandy-brown hair was cropped close and his black suit scarcely looked like barista wear.

"Sam," the man held out his hand. "I've moved back too."

"Who are you?" Sam squinted.

"Chris, your old classmate. Don't you remember?" He made eye contact with Raquel and she almost sank through the wood chair.

This was Chris? And he wasn't being rude at all about her standing him up. She'd find him an exceptionally nice blind date to make it up to him.

"Chris, long time. What are you up to, man?" Sam took a swig of coffee.

Unasked, Chris pulled up a chair. He was all too close to Raquel's side of the table. His lanky legs touched her calves when he stretched back.

"I'm a doctor now." Chris's hand rested on the table.

Wow, how had she missed that?

"Just did a three year stint with Doctors Without Borders. Treated Ebola patients in Africa."

Her jaw dropped.

"Glad to be back in the U.S., though. I got a job as head of research at the cancer lab downtown. We'll be working on new treatments for lung cancer."

Sam whistled. "What's that pay?"

"Sam!" Raquel bit her tongue. Chiding Sam wasn't going to procure her a second date.

Chris's lips twisted into a smile as he shrugged. "Enough. What are you doing these days?"

"I was Special Forces. Been to countries you haven't even heard of. But now," Sam glanced down to his leg. The cast had come off since he'd stopped by. "This bum leg got me discharged."

"Do you have a job?"

Sam shook his head.

"Won't the Veterans Affairs office get you one?" Raquel stopped studying the scratches on the table. "It's on TV all the time how the President is helping veterans."

She didn't mind that he was unemployed, but he was traditional enough that there was no chance he'd propose until after he found a job.

Sam guffawed. "That communist? Our vets are all scrubbing toilets and putting out job applications. Average unemployment is two years."

Her heart sank.

"I have a job if you want it." Chris's black shoes rested on the table trestle. "Head of operations. You keep the lab from being broken into and manage the security and hazardous waste team. Not terribly exciting, but it pays 60k a year."

"Wow, I . . ." Sam looked uncomfortable.

"You should take it. At least temporarily." Raquel's fingers pressed around the cinnamon shaker. This would be perfect.

"You're right." Sam looked at Chris. "I'll take it."

"Wonderful. I'll let our manager know." Chris stood.

He was leaving and she could focus her attention on Sam. So why didn't she feel happier? Refusing to watch Chris's receding back, Raquel made eye contact with Sam. His eyes were brown, dirty brown. Chris's were blue.

"I was going to wait, Raquel." Sam extracted a small package from his pocket. "But since we're celebrating my new job anyway...."

She blushed as he shoved the present towards her. "Thank you." Her fingers tugged the red silk ribbon. Shiny green paper tore.

The lid of the box swung up on a hinge. Raquel gasped.

A diamond ring stared out of a black velvet box.

Sam leaned back against the leather booth, hands behind his head. "Marry me?"

A marriage proposal? Today? She should have ordered a coffee first. Her tongue felt dry enough to stick to the roof her mouth.

A cough came from behind Sam's head. Chris stood there, a newly purchased cup of coffee in his hands. "I know this is atrocious timing. But I have to tell you something before you agree to be his wife."

Chris stepped around the booth, towards her. "I've loved you ever since second grade, when you gave me that Hershey kiss. The reason I wanted to take you out to dinner yesterday was to ask if you'd be my girlfriend."

Two men fighting over her: every girl's dream. Only it was much more awkward than she'd imagined. Raquel's hands fidgeted.

Smile flipping into a frown, Sam straightened to upright. His glance at Chris wasn't friendly. "You're not going to take away my job when she says yes, are you?"

"Of course not." Chris turned away. His shoes clapped against the tile floor.

"All right then, Raquel. Let's try this on for size." Sam circled the table to Raquel's side. "We could have a Christmas wedding."

Instinctively, her hand drew back. "I need to think Sam. Chris just asked me—"

"Chris?" Sam snorted. "You've always been in love with me. My sister said you moped like a heartbroken nun these last four years I've been gone."

"You knew that's how I felt and you still didn't come back?" Tears formed in her eyes. Christmas Eve four years ago had been sheer misery.

"I loved the job more, but that's not a choice anymore. We'll do it all like you wanted, the two story house, white picket fence." Sam's hand rested on the back of her chair, arm almost encircling her.

"No!" She stood.

Sam halted, ring gripped between his thick fingers.

"I'm not marrying anyone," she stated. "I'll go out on dates with you. And I'll go out on dates with whoever else I want. And in a couple of months, I'll decide who I like best."

"Don't be ridiculous. I already dated you." Sam's hand dropped to his side.

"Eight years ago and then you left and chose the job." Raquel pressed her arms tighter against her chest, even though it did rumple her new Macy's blouse.

"So?" Sam's hand flipped, palm up.

"I want to be dated properly."

"No way. I picked you because you were the easy option, already in love with me. If I have to actually date someone, I'm going to sign up for e-harmony." Sam shoved the ring back into his pocket.

And she didn't care. Her high heels hit the tile at a run. The door chimes tinkled as she burst out of the door. "Chris."

Several yards ahead of her, he walked swiftly, head down. Snow had begun to fall and the shoulders of his suit had already caught a light dusting.

"Chris!" Tearing off her heels, she ran across the icy pavement in her pantyhose. Her hand caught his arm. "Chris, I want to go to dinner with you."

He twisted around. "You do?"

The Circadian was the best restaurant in town. Candles flickered, setting the mood, and a fireplace crackled behind them.

Raquel's knife sliced through the salmon, but her gaze was on Chris.

He dabbled in art too. He'd even painted a mosaic down in the Liberian compound he had helped construct.

The waiter cleared the plates and brought dessert.

Now Chris was telling her that he'd illegally downloaded all of Mumford and Son's albums because he was too impatient to wait for them to be shipped to Africa.

She really should have read his emails these last four years.

"That was the day the pride of lions stalked the head of surgery and me."

"Go on." Her fork lay neglected with the delicious gingerbread cake barely touched.

"I don't want to bore you. I already told you that story."

"No, you didn't." She smiled and hoped her lipstick hadn't been completely worn off by the salmon.

"Yeah, I emailed you the whole thing last month."

"Oh, I . . ." she looked down at the carpeted floor, "never read your emails."

"But you replied."

"I, um, kind of treated it like a journal." She held her cloth napkin up to shield her face.

He laughed. His blue eyes twinkled when he did that. "So I know everything about you and you know nothing about me. I like this."

"Not quite everything." She tilted her shoulder.

He looked at her. His big hands were on the table. She could imagine them performing surgery, stitching up hearts, and cutting out appendixes.

"Yes," his voice had a melodic tone.

"You don't know it, but I'm planning to say yes when you ask me to be your girlfriend."

"You are?" He didn't even breath, just stared at her.

"Yes." Leaning over the narrow table, her hand slid over his.

His lips looked supremely kiss-worthy. How had she not noticed that in high school? Her gaze slid from his eyes to his lips. She angled closer.

"Nice guys don't kiss girls on the first date."

Her face flamed with heat. She jerked back from the table. But his fingers had closed over hers.

"On the other hand, we have been corresponding for four years."

His eyes sparkled with a teasing light. She liked it.

"True," she moved around the table to his side. His hand still clasped her left. Even sitting, his head came up past her shoulders.

His thumb traced a circle around her fourth finger. "And I fully intend to do everything in my power to get a ring on that finger by Christmas time next year."

"Oh, do you now?" Bending forward, she let her lips just graze his. The scent of aromatic coffee clung to his white dress shirt.

His mouth closed over hers. The fragrance of holly berries and cinnamon strands and gingerbread dessert all rolled into one as she closed her eyes.

"I love Christmas," she whispered.

About the Author

Anne Garboczi Evans holds a Master's in Counseling and Bachelor's in Classical Liberal Arts. She has had a passion for writing historical fiction ever since reading Rosemary Sutcliff's novels as a preteen. She wrote her first full length novel at fifteen. She is a military spouse and mother to a little boy, "Joe-Joe."

Her inspiration for Hot Lead and Cold Apple Pie came from moving to the Colorado Rockies. She loves reading Christian fiction and wanted to weave a lighthearted tale about love, rivalry, and the taming of the west.

When not writing, you can find Anne reading Dr. Seuss for the 100th time, vainly attempting to potty train Joe-Joe, or working on her fixer-upper house with her husband.

You can find her online at:

http://annegarboczievans.com/

http://annegarboczievans.blogspot.com/

https://www.facebook.com/annegarboczievans

https://twitter.com/garboczievans

the Christmas Gift

KAREN WINGATE

*J*en Huckabee brushed her hand across the cold condensation collecting on her living room window, and then rubbed a dripping hand on her jeans. Peering through the cleared spot, she let out a sigh heavy with longing and anxiety. The only thing right about this Christmas morning was the snow-swept landscape of the high Colorado plateau outside her window, a backdrop for the town where Keith ministered to a struggling congregation. The view looked like a Thomas Kincaid moment.

A raucous cough sounded from the back of the house, releasing her look on the picture perfect view. Letting the recycled handmade white eyelet curtains fall, she rubbed her damp hand across her face. If only it took that tiny of a gesture to brush aside the exhaustion of the last few days.

What was that line in their marriage vows? In sickness and in health? If someone had told her the sickness part would include missing Christmas because of one sick husband and two sick babies, she may have reconsidered the deal.

It was their second Christmas in Colorado, hundreds of miles from extended family in Georgia and Arizona. Keith had made the most of it, telling her they were free to make their own memories. Katie and Leah were now two and four, the perfect ages to catch the magic of Christmas. The meager salary of their first ministry didn't give much wiggle room, but they had spent what they could to make this Christmas one for the record books. Debbie and Terry, church members who were quickly becoming friends, had invited them to spend Christmas dinner with them for the second year in a row.

"Please don't bring anything." Debbie was adamant when Jen asked what she could contribute to The Big Feast, as Leah liked to call it. "My mother and I have our menu all planned."

It didn't seem right not to cook something on Christmas Day, so Jen had spent weeks dreaming and planning a lavish brunch, filled with all the good things preschoolers and Keith's southern taste-buds would enjoy, enough food to hold them until the Big Feast later that afternoon.

Jen had spelled out her perfect Christmas Day to a patient Keith as they cuddled on the couch one frosty evening a week ago. "We'll open presents first, I'll put the finishing touches on breakfast, we'll eat leisurely with no need to rush off to anything, and then we'll play with Christmas presents until we have to leave for Deb and Terry's."

Keith looked up at the digital thermometer. "It's ten below zero."

She punched him with a pillow. "You're not listening!"

"I am too. You want a big breakfast and I get to play with my toys until we leave for Deb and Terry's."

"No, silly. You're Daddy. You have to put together Leah's dollhouse."

"You mean I can't play with the new electric drill you got me?"

She stood up, drawing her sweater around her. "You peeked!"

He grinned. "Nope. Leah told me."

If this was any foretaste of what their Christmas would be like, it was going to be wonderful.

It was not to be.

After living eighteen months in the high alpine valley of Southern Colorado known for resilient strep throat viruses, they had thought their little family would be acclimated to the harsh weather of a Rocky Mountain winter. Twenty below zero nights and a drafty house that caused one-inch thick ice buildup on the inside of the windows meant frequent trips to the doctor and more money doled out for prescriptions than for food.

Jen wasn't about to give up on her dream Christmas. Even after a restless night of holding two-year-old Katie and poking cough syrup down the others, there would still be Christmas. She set the table, spread out enough dishes to rival any breakfast bar and woke the family with a cheery, "Merry Christmas!"

The light and wonder of Christmas had fled from their eyes. Katie held her head in her hand and Leah coughed a deep gurgling rattle while staring at the box that held her new dollhouse. Jen put away the lavish uneaten breakfast then stood at the window, her shoulder muscles aching with fatigue. There would be no holiday spent with friends that year.

She trudged down the hall and opened the bedroom door. "You all right?"

Keith pulled the covers to his chin. Katie coughed into his side. "We're as fine as can be, I suppose." His voice was thin, not the beautiful deep bass voice she had fallen in love with not so many years ago in the seminary library.

Keith turned his head away from Katie and sniffled. "Our family can't be satisfied to catch only what everybody else has, can we?"

Jen held out her fingers. "Strep throat, sinus infection, ear infection, and bronchitis." She counted them off. "I didn't know anyone could get all those ailments at one time. Much less all three of you."

"It's amazing you aren't sick."

The grin she forced across her face actually hurt. "I can't afford to be sick. Someone has to take care of the rest of you."

"I thought you would say you're too ornery." His yawn ended in a cough. "I'm sorry I'm not more help to you."

She kissed his feverish forehead. "Sweetie, you are helping. Katie is a lot calmer here in bed with you."

"Have you checked on Leah?"

Jen looked toward the closed bedroom door across the hall. "No, but I don't like that gurgle in her chest. She could have pneumonia. We may have to go back to the doctor tomorrow."

"Have you called Deb yet to tell her we can't come?" His voice was sleepy.

She sighed, wishing she could put off the inevitable. "No, not yet."

The ice of social acceptability grew thinner the more she waited, yet she didn't want to admit to anyone, especially to church members that the pastor's family was so sick. Pastors were supposed to be strong for everyone else, weren't they? They were never to be sick and if they were, they weren't supposed to mention it. They were to meet everyone else's needs, not have any needs of their own.

She wasn't sure where she had heard that line of poppycock and in her head, she knew it wasn't true. Still, it was hard to admit that her family was so sick. She could see old Mrs. Owen's scowl and furrowed forehead as she lectured Jen on how she wasn't covering the baby well enough to protect her from the harsh Colorado cold. In other words, if your family is sick, it's your fault.

Deb and Terry aren't like that.

She was too exhausted to believe the truth, too worried to argue. She heaved another sigh. If deep breaths cleared the lungs of bacterial minions, all her sighing that morning should boost her immune system a hundredfold. Jen headed for her cell phone.

"I'm so sorry Keith and the girls are sick." Deb sounded entirely too chipper. "Don't worry at all about not coming. It's all right. You take care of that little family of yours. Really, Jen, it's okay."

Jen punched the red button on her Smartphone. Church members could be so superficial. What else could Deb say but the proper thing? All twenty families in their small congregation would know by nightfall that the pastor and his family were sick in bed. If any of the Huckabees made it to church next Sunday, she was sure to get an earful from Mrs. Owen.

Jen opened the refrigerator and stared at the round cartons of scrambled eggs and sausage gravy. Now that they weren't going anywhere for Christmas dinner, what could she fix? What did it matter? She would be the only one to eat or care about eating. What was so important about Christmas dinner anyway when her family was so sick?

Leah's cry sped Jen's feet down the hallway. She picked up the child and collapsed in the rattan rocker left over from days of nursing the babies. The sight of Leah's small pallid face laying so still in her arms filled Jen's chest with an ache of love and fear. "Lord, keep me well so I can take care of them!"

She was alone. She was responsible for these three very sick people, yet cut off from the rest of the world because it was Christmas Day. Everyone else was absorbed in their own family celebrations. Who would want to hear her whine about her dismal day? Who could she call on if any of them got worse?

A rap so soft she would have missed it if Leah hadn't been so still sounded at the front of the house. She stood, placed Leah in her bed, and shuffled to the front door. There it was again.

Terry stood on the snowy doorstep balancing four foil wrapped paper plates, each tied with green ribbon, and the top plate bearing a white envelope. "Deb insisted I bring this over to you. It's your Christmas dinner."

"Terry! You shouldn't have." If she cried, the intense cold would immediately freeze the tears to her cheek.

He shrugged and waved off her protest. "God gave me what I needed at Christmas. Seems like the least we could do." With a quick "Merry Christmas," he was back inside his warm car.

Closing the door against the cold, Jen lifted the foil from one plate and breathed in the succulent steam from pork loin, gourmet mashed potatoes, and green beans amandine. A cherry nut salad, her favorite, made the plate attractive enough to take top billing at a Paula Dean cooking show.

Storing the other three plates in the fridge, Jen stood at the kitchen counter, savoring each bite. She set down her fork and removed a gorgeous Christmas card from the gold foil envelope. The beautiful expressions of love from Deb, Terry, and Deb's parents made worries of the morning seem silly and unfounded.

"Call us if you need *anything*." Deb's underlined message created a lump so large Jen wondered if she was catching the strep throat virus.

They weren't alone. Someone cared. God, through His people, had showered their family with love and faithfulness. The same way God filled the manger with a tiny baby so many years ago. Because the world needed it.

It was a different sort of Christmas. But it was still a Christmas for the record books.

About the Author

For over twenty-five years, Karen Wingate wrote Christian education curriculum for several companies and over two hundred articles for such magazines as Guidposts, Decision, Clubhouse, and The Lookout. She has completed two novels and is busy working on more fiction projects and her blog at www.graceonparade.com/blog. After working with churches in five other states including Colorado, Karen and her husband Jack now minister to a congregation in rural Illinois. They have two adult daughters and are owned by a Welsh Corgi.

You can find Karen online at:

www.graceonparade.com

https://www.facebook.com/graceonparade?ref=bookmarks

https://twitter.com/kwingate715

Love is the Key

APRIL STRAUCH

ourtney walked slowly through Hampton's Home for the Elderly, careful not to jiggle the package. On the way to Miss Ava's room, she passed a nine-foot Douglas Fir, covered with gold and silver ornaments. Pine boughs, laden with red berries and strung popcorn, draped the Great Room fireplace. Figurines of Santa, and snowmen, lined bookshelves and coffee tables. Burl Ives', *Holly Jolly Christmas*, played softly from the vintage phonograph in the foyer. She paused to peek in the Recreation Room where residents tapped their feet and sipped hot apple cider.

"Good morning." Courtney swung a blonde braid over her shoulder and hid the gift bag by the closet. "If you take your medicine, I have a surprise for you."

Miss Ava, Courtney's favorite resident, turned 88 years-old last month. Her routine was the same each morning: sit in the brown recliner and read the Bible. Pray aloud, at imperceptible decibels. Intermittently, fidget with a tiny, gold key necklace.

This morning, Courtney frowned when she found Miss Ava asleep in her chair. The past few days the older woman talked slower than normal and had developed a cough. Her ankles swelled daily.

Courtney put the symptoms out of her mind.

So as not to disturb her, Courtney dusted. A bureau, single bed, and small television were the only furniture in the room. Propped on the dresser was a faded photo of Miss Ava's late husband, Richard. Courtney noticed his winsome smile each time she cleaned. He stood in the woods, clad in a black and red checked flannel jacket. Was this taken in the 60s or 70s?

Courtney picked up the picture frame and peered closely. Funny, she never noticed the small tow-headed boy who peaked around the woodpile. She made a mental note to ask Miss Ava about him. Returning the photo to the dresser, she dropped it. Flustered, she propped it back up, thankful the glass didn't break.

"Why hello, dear." Miss Ava raised her head and blinked rapidly. "Is it that time already?" She shook her head. "I must have dozed off."

"That's all right, we all need rest." Courtney smiled and walked across the room.

"How's my favorite nurse today?"

Courtney poured water into a glass and placed two small pills in Miss Ava's hand. "*Soon to be* nurse. I still have two more semesters to go."

The old woman's hands shook as she put the pills in her mouth. She swallowed hard and struggled to catch her breath. "They stick in my throat." She coughed for a full thirty seconds and then spoke with a rasp. "Well, if you ask me, young people today are too busy. It's too much for a body."

Courtney grinned and fluffed the pillow behind Miss Ava's head. "Oh, I don't mind being busy. It keeps my mind occupied."

"There now, pills are down the hatch." Miss Ava's voice sounded stronger. "Where's this surprise you promised?"

Courtney walked across the carpet and retrieved the present. For a split second, she froze. What made her think she could do this? Trent told her it was the right thing. Now, she wasn't so sure. When Miss Ava opened the bag to discover the two-foot ceramic Christmas tree, Courtney knew she had made a good decision.

Miss Ava clapped her hands. "Oh, how beautiful!" She cradled the tree in her hands, turning it this way and that, until she inspected every inch. "Plug it in, won't you?"

Courtney displayed the heirloom on the dresser and knelt down beside Miss Ava's chair. Tiny green and red lights twinkled while the tree swiveled to the tune of, *Oh Christmas Tree.* For a moment neither of them spoke.

"Look, Miss Ava." Courtney pointed to the window. "It's snowing."

"Well, I'll be! A Christmas surprise." Miss Ava flung her hands in the air. "A present. Now snow. You can't imagine how all this warms an old woman's heart."

Miss Ava touched Courtney's shoulder. "Sincerely, I thank you."

Courtney beamed. "Thank *you.* There's no one else I would rather enjoy it. You don't have any other decorations. I thought it might spruce things up."

She'd never talked to Miss Ava about her lack of visitors. She didn't want to pry. Once, Miss Ava told her she was an only child. And a widow. Still, it pained Courtney to see someone so alone. There was a time she herself felt like the very gates of heaven closed on her.

"Now, tell me, where did you find something so special?" Miss Ava reached for her water glass.

"My mother painted it," Courtney said quietly.

"Oh, I see," Miss Ava whispered and lowered her gaze. "I should have guessed." Her voice cracked and she coughed again. "She certainly was a talented painter."

Courtney bent down by the recliner.

"I don't know what I would've done without you these past two years, Miss Ava. Losing Mom and Dad was the hardest thing in the world." Now, her own voice trembled and she shivered. "You never gave up on me. All those weeks I barely spoke to you. I'm so ashamed. I just didn't know what to do with my grief."

"There, there." Miss Ava patted her on the shoulder. "I prayed hard, child. The Lord holds our time in His hands." She wiped her eyes. "Sorrow takes time to heal."

"I thought God forgot me." Courtney bowed her head and the tears fell.

Memories pounded against her brain.

Her, sitting at the table while her 10 year-old twin sisters whimpered on her lap. Her phone call with the police. A double funeral two days after Christmas. Anger when the drunk driver received only a five year sentence. Then numbness, perhaps the worst of all. She spent weeks in her pajamas staring out the window. Until she came to work here. And met Trent at the University.

"You told me never to give in to despair, Miss Ava. To trust God had a plan in all the pain."

"Courtney, you mustn't thank me. There's so much you don't understand." Her voice broke.

"Oh, Miss Ava, how can I not thank you? You've spent hours listening, and helping me work through the horror of the accident. Why, I didn't even sleep for months because of grief and anxiety. Until talking things through with you, I had no peace. You've…" She faltered. "You've been like a mother when I needed one most."

"Courtney, life isn't always as it seems. And you are stronger than you think." She sat up straighter. "In the Christmas season, we must remind each other of the gift our Lord gave us. Without His Son, we would all be hopeless."

Suddenly, Miss Ava stopped talking and wrung her hands together. She closed her eyes and fingered the gold key.

Courtney didn't want to intrude on her friend's solitude. But after all the intense emotions it was good to concentrate on something else.

"Miss Ava." She tapped the old woman on her shoulder.

"Yes?" Miss Ava opened her eyes slowly. "Bring me the picture, won't you? From the dresser."

Courtney carefully removed the frame and brought it to Miss Ava.

"Do you see this little boy here, behind Richard?"

"Yes, he looks just like his father." She glanced at Miss Ava. "But he has your eyes."

"Our son, Franklin. Everyone called him Frankie. When he was but a wee lad, he carried around a little cedar chest. I believe I got it with green stamps. Or maybe it was the antique store on the corner." She waved her hand. "No matter. Well, he put all his treasures in it. One time, rocks. Another time, flower petals." She laughed. "And once, he brought me a frog. Boy, I nigh about jumped out of my skin." The wrinkles on her face, made her eyes disappear.

She reached for her neck. "This key goes to that box."

Silence.

Wasn't she going to tell Courtney where the box was? What was in it now? And why she continued to wear the key? Miss Ava remained silent, her eyes closed.

Courtney wondered if she might be remembering Christmases of long ago. Perhaps sweet times with Richard and Frankie. The three of them gathered around the tree Christmas morning? Or, eating ham and cranberry stuffing?

"He was a good boy, he was." As Miss Ava spoke, a tear slipped down her cheek. She coughed again and stayed silent.

"Where is he now?" Courtney was afraid to ask, but curiosity won the battle.

"Far away from here. From me. And his Heavenly Father." Miss Ava closed her eyes. It was a long while before she spoke.

"Life doesn't always turn out the way we think. But all things work for good for them that love the Lord."

Courtney couldn't help herself. She leaned over and hugged Miss Ava for a long embrace.

Miss Ava took a deep breath. "Enough of this seriousness. Now, I want to hear all about that man of yours. If I have my facts straight, and I usually do, shouldn't we be talking about your upcoming wedding?"

Courtney's voice raised a notch. "I can't believe I'm getting married in five days."

"This will be the last time I see you before you are a married woman." Miss Ava nodded.

Courtney laughed. "Oh, Miss Ava, you sure are something. You have quite a memory for..."

"For someone my age." Her eyes twinkled.

For the next half hour, Courtney helped Miss Ava with her exercises, cleaned her room, and talked non-stop about Trent, the love of her life. She totally forgot about a long ago photo, and a little boy's box.

Every Tuesday night Courtney and Trent ate at the local sub shop while the twins were at ballet.

As she savored her spinach salad with warm bacon dressing, Courtney told Trent about the tree she had given Miss Ava.

Courtney wiped her mouth. "You were right. "

"Aren't I always?" Trent leaned back in the booth.

"What?"

"Right, silly." His eyes sparkled and he chuckled.

"Well, it was really hard at first to think of giving it away. I mean, Mom painted it. Dad loved it. Giving it to her today...I don't know how to explain it. It was as if I relinquished a part of me. I've moved on from the accident. As much as possible, that is. Yet, I can't escape the feeling there's more to it."

She laughed. "You know me, always thinking too much. Guess it comes from Mom being a psychologist and Dad a social worker. What a combo I am, right?" She took a bite of her garlic bread.

"That's why I love you." Trent leaned forward.

"Because we're polar opposites?" She smiled. "My engineering fiancée who looks at life like a math problem. A+B=C, no need for purpose or knowing the 'why'."

"I love you for many reasons."

Trent's smile still made her heart flutter. She could hardly fathom by the end of the week, she and Trent would be man and wife.

He leaned back. "No, seriously. You've been dealt a hard situation. Losing your parents. Raising Emily and Hannah. But most of all, moving on from the anger at the injustice of it all."

"Before you give me too much credit, I should tell you something." She worked her lip. "For the last several weeks I've just been scared."

Trent looked worried. "About getting married? Only five days to change your mind."

"No." She reached for his hands. "At least not in the way you think."

"I'm not following." He furrowed his eyebrows and his head tilted.

Courtney sighed and rested her chin in her hands. She gazed around the restaurant where her parents brought her as a child.

"See these blue and white checkered curtains? The Christmas tree with blue lights right in front of the window? And the Santa waving out front?"

Trent raised one eyebrow.

"It's all the same as when I was a kid. This restaurant is a constant in this town. But what if it burned to the ground?"

Trent fiddled with the string on his hoodie. "Ok?"

"Things change in an instant, Trent. Here today, gone tomorrow. Just like Mom and Dad. This morning I told Miss Ava I was afraid if I married you, I might lose you too."

Trent's eyes softened. "Guess I might feel the same way if I'd gone through what you have." He reached across the table and stroked her cheek. "I can't promise you I'll never die, or get sick, or be in an accident. But I can promise you, I'll always love you. And the twins. Love is what matters most."

Courtney smiled. "That's just about verbatim what Miss Ava told me too. About love being the most important."

Trent leaned forward again and looked at his watch. "Hey, I have an idea. The girls don't get out of ballet for another hour." He reached for their coats in the booth. "Miss Ava sounds like a pretty wise woman. And in all this time you've worked at Hampton's, I've never met this angel in disguise. Do you think she could handle meeting your Prince Charming?"

Courtney pulled on her coat and kissed Trent on the cheek. "I think she'd love it."

Ava Michaels asked the nighttime nurse to keep Courtney's Christmas tree plugged in as she fell asleep. Her room was dark, except for the glow of the red and green twinkling lights.

As she lay in bed, Ava went over the evening in her mind. What a wonderful surprise visit she enjoyed with Courtney and Trent. It was a pleasure getting to know the young man Courtney was to marry in just a few, short days.

Ava took note of the sweet way Trent gazed at Courtney as she spoke. It touched a deep place in Ava's heart. This young couple reminded her of herself and Richard, many years ago. How she missed him!

A sudden coughing fit broke the peaceful quietness. Ava reached for her water glass on the dresser. It slipped from her hand like a wriggling fish.

Crash!

She was embarrassed when staff members came running. They were so polite while they picked up shards of glass, making sure every last speck was cleared from the carpet. Concern appeared on their faces, though.

Time was running out. She felt strength go from her body each day. But her mind was so alive! She groaned. "Lord, show me what to do."

She closed her eyes, but slept restlessly, and dreamed of bull frogs and daises. And a small, cedar box.

Abruptly at 2:00 a.m., she awoke. With strength she didn't know she had, she slipped from under the covers and walked across the room to her recliner. Tucked in her knitting bag, under several skeins of yarn, was the box.

Ever so quietly, she opened it. Five letters.

She reached up to turn on the light by the chair. Hopefully no nurse passing by would stop to check on her. She needed some time alone.

Her tears flowed freely as she read each letter and then carefully tucked them back into the envelopes. The return address was the same on all five. Frankie Michaels. His name, followed by an inmate number.

She balled her hands into fists. Reducing her precious boy to a number like items on a grocery list. He had a soul! He had a mother!

Suddenly she knew what to do.

For the next hour she wrote a letter back to him. Telling him how much she loved him. How God still had a plan for his life and not to lose hope. Words came to her mind faster than she could write. She coughed several times, but kept working. After writing to Frankie, she pulled out one more piece of stationary. This time her words came slower. Tears sprang to her eyes and her hands shook. Finally, the last line written, she folded the paper. Unexplainable peace descended on her soul. She leaned back in the chair and fingered the key on her neck.

Sudden pain ripped through her chest. She tried to call for help, but no sound came. She gripped the armrests of the chair and tried speaking. All she mustered was shallow breaths. The room spun. Such pressure on her chest.

The last thing she saw was a ceramic Christmas tree with twinkling red and green lights.

Then, her pen dropped to the floor.

Courtney couldn't believe how fast the week went after the wedding. She and Trent went to the Cayman Islands for a three-day honeymoon. The rest of the week, they took the girls to Disney World for a whirlwind vacation.

Although Courtney and her sisters had sad moments remembering their parent's death, they were thrilled to start this new chapter in their lives. Now, they all looked forward to Christmas. Only two days away.

Courtney ran down the hall and into Miss Ava's room.

"I'm back! I brought you something. You're gonna love it." She reached her arm around the door to put her present by the closet.

"What are you staring at?"

An old man's gravelly voice made Courtney do a double take. He sat in a wheelchair and Wheel of Fortune blared from the TV. On his lap was a green army blanket. Only one leg rested on the metal step of the chair.

"Where's my coffee," he snapped. "How long does it take to make coffee in this place?"

Courtney's heart pounded. Miss Ava's brown recliner was gone. The dresser and the picture frame were nowhere to be seen.

She ran to the nurses' station.

"Where's Miss Ava?" She panted and bent over, hands on her knees.

Eileen, the charge nurse, looked up from her computer monitor. "I tried calling you." Her eyes softened. "You were on your honeymoon. I didn't want to intrude."

Courtney grabbed onto the ledge of the station. "Please. Tell me what's going on. Who is that man in Miss Ava's room?"

An hour later, Courtney was back home in her living room. Eileen had explained Miss Ava had a heart attack. She hadn't suffered.

Eileen gave Courtney the rest of the day off. The supervisor sent her home with apologies and the ceramic tree. Also, a brown bag with Courtney's name scrawled on the side. The staff had found it by Miss Ava's brown recliner. Inside was the cedar box and tiny key necklace.

Courtney called Trent, and he came home from work. He sat by her now on the couch.

"Are you all right?" He rubbed her back.

She smiled at him through tears. "Miss Ava was old and I knew her health was declining. I'm so glad I got to know her," she said softly.

Courtney's hands shook when she opened the box lid to find the letters from Franklin Michaels. On the bottom of the stack, lay a letter addressed to her. She read aloud.

Dearest Courtney,

I pray you won't hold it against me for not telling you. My son, Frankie, is the drunk driver who killed your parents."

Courtney gasped and grabbed Trent's arm.

When I was transferred to Hampton's Home for the Elderly to be closer to Frankie, I prayed God would grant me a way to reach my son.

He was born to Richard and me late in life. 'A blessing in disguise', Richard used to call him. Frankie was such a good boy, Courtney—still is. He got on a wrong path and never quite found his way back.

It didn't take me long to know you were my miracle.

"I can't do this." Courtney clenched her fists.

Trent gently took the letter from her. In his strong voice, he read on.

"You've talked about me giving you hope. My dear girl, you gave an old woman with a broken heart the desire to carry on. The Lord himself ministered to me through your kind ways and precious gift.

My time is short, Courtney. I need your help.

Trent squeezed Courtney's hand. "Do you want me to go on?" She nodded.

"In this box are the letters from Frankie. He wrote them to me, from prison. He's searching, and he needs what you have.

Tell him about the miracle of Christmas. About the Son who saves all who believe...."

"That's all. The end of the letter." Trent turned the page over. "Seems like she wanted to say something more, but the words trail off." He pointed to the page.

Courtney's throat burned and she gritted her teeth. Suddenly, she jumped off the couch and paced back and forth. It was too much to ask. The pain was too deep.

Then she remembered the tree.

Giving it up to Miss Ava brought healing. What had she said to Trent that night in the sub shop—that she knew there was a reason to move on from the accident?

Now, she knew what she was moving on to.

Forgiveness.

"Can you do it? Offer comfort to someone who hurt you so badly?" Trent rubbed his chin.

Courtney felt something brush against her leg. The small necklace had slipped from the bag. The same one Miss Ava wore every day. She picked it up and laid it carefully in her palm.

Nodding slowly to Trent, she spoke through her tears.

"With God's help."

Courtney gently opened the clasp and slipped it around her own neck.

She gazed into Trent's eyes. "For every circumstance, for every pain we endure, there's hope."

Then she leaned her head on his shoulder, already praying for words to give to Miss Ava's son. "If God brought Miss Ava into my life in such a miraculous way," she said, "I believe anything is possible." She fingered the necklace.

"No matter what, His love is always the key."

About the Author

April Strauch is the author of Lilac Lessons, a devotional book on adoption. Her work has also been published in *Today's Christian Woman*, *The Secret Place*, and countless other magazines. She lives in Northeastern PA with her husband and two middle-school age daughters, both born in China. April is a secretary with ARS Enterprises, a computer business she and her husband have owned for over 20 years. She also works part-time in a law office. April's hope is that her writing draws readers into a closer relationship with God and causes them to seek Him for answers to life's hard questions.

April enjoys spending time with her family, crocheting, and walking on country roads lined with corn fields.

April Strauch - Author of Lilac Lessons, A Journey Through All Stages of Adoption

You can find April online at www.aprilstrauch.com and on Facebook: http://www.facebook.com/April.Strauch

the Forever Christmas Gift

ELAINE STOCK

$\mathcal{N}$evaeh crossed San Francisco's busy California Street. She tuned out the quacking honks of the rush hour traffic and did what she did best: releasing her imagination. *I'm back home, in Maine. The icy cold fingers of winter are wrapping around my ankles. Nearby, a frozen tree branch creaks from its heavy blanket of snow.* Reaching the safety of the city sidewalk, Nevaeh became aware, again, that not only was she miles away from her family but the cold of loneliness still nipped at her heart.

A metallic clang summoned her attention toward the department store before her. Festive Christmas wreaths decorated the doors. Glittery silver and blue tinsel swags draped the display-windows, one with a mannequin girl sitting on Santa's lap and the other showing a storybook-like village, complete with Santa's sleigh and reindeer traversing its midnight sky. Everyone needed a bit of cheer during the often-stressful holidays. She knew she did.

Standing before the store's entrance a bell ringer for the Salvation Army rang up a symphony for contributions to his apple-red kettle. He greeted each passerby with such warmth that it was as if he knew the women and men on a personal basis. Dressed in green corduroy pants, a yellow and blue plaid shirt poking out from his red pullover sweater, and with a white fuzzy scarf wrapped around his neck, the man appeared to not favor one color over the other. Nevaeh would have judged him as either theatrical, or if she kept with her adolescent moodiness of only a few years ago, as a bit freaky. Whoever he was, he certainly worked his magic. People shoved hands into pockets and purses and whipped out dollar bills. Nevaeh grew wide-eyed when a white-haired lady dressed in ragged clothing handed him a twenty-dollar bill.

"Thank you kindly, miss," the bell-ringer said. "God bless you." He then glanced at Nevaeh, smiled, and motioned her over.

She wanted to pull the hood of her rain slicker over her head and disappear. How embarrassing.

"Nevaeh," the ringer called.

Nevaeh blinked. Russell? Her next-door neighbor in apartment 4-C? She hadn't recognized him. That's what she got for leaving her glasses behind at work. Russell was way older than her parents—had to be at least in his late sixties or early seventies. He was always pleasant with his cheerful good-mornings and snippets of conversations as they shared an elevator ride down to the building's lobby on their way to work. She was forever trying to avoid him. No luck this time.

"Hello, Nevaeh, my friendly nursery school assistant."

Nevaeh gave a little wave of her fingers. "Hi, Russell. I didn't know you volunteered."

"It's the very least I can do."

Nevaeh absently nodded as she pictured him hunched over upright and grand pianos, tuning them for customers' fancy holiday parties or family get-togethers. He didn't have much of a family, only a nephew living in Anchorage and a career-Army niece stationed somewhere in Africa. Instead of questioning God about the why-nots in life, Russell told her that he accepted God's grace and blessings each day and tried to glorify Him by being a good servant. Russell was big on God.

A sigh swirled inside Nevaeh. Someone had to get the God thingy, she guessed. Her parents sure didn't. They stayed as far away from a church as they could get, clinking wine glasses in a toast to their one hundred wooded acres of sheer privacy. They gloated about their success, that their self-made paradise was the closest to heaven they'd ever achieve. Maybe that's why they named her what they did.

She eyed the red donation pot. "Having good results?"

"Yes. And I have to admit—it's lifting up my tired soul."

"Tired?" She licked her lips, wondering if she was gabbing too much. Past experiences had taught her that the less said, the safer she'd likely be.

He gave a half chuckle, half groan. "My young friend, I hope you never grow weary from the day's disappointments."

As if it were only the two of them discussing the latest news while riding in the elevator or exchanging a muffled hello in the basement laundry room, Nevaeh straightened with alert and concern for her neighbor. Maybe Russell experienced similar things as she did, despite their age differences. Maybe he wasn't the silly, over-friendly nuisance she thought she had to put up with on occasion.

She rubbed an ear.

"What?" he asked, but held his smile.

"I'd never box you into the category of weary. You seem so . . . alive. I'll turn twenty-one in January and I wish I had your energy. Giving away your secrets?"

"I'll tell you what." Russell glanced at his watch. "My shift ends in a half hour. I can meet you at seven this evening back at the apartment, and if you like, we could attend a worship service at my church." Perhaps to emphasize it, Russell glanced upward. "It's very informal—God loves us no matter how we're dressed."

By the lift of a brow and a twinkle in his eyes, she could tell that he noticed her examining his clothes.

He chuckled. "Or, a colorful attire."

She smiled. Because of him. And she liked him a bit more because of that.

Nevaeh looked down at the sidewalk. "I'm not into God. Much."

"Much, huh? Well, God's into you. Always."

She sidestepped away. "I have to go now."

"Nevaeh?"

Nevaeh had been poised to turn and walk away but when she heard the kindness in his voice she faced him.

"How about tomorrow, for the Christmas Eve service?"

"You go to church a lot."

Russell smiled, stretching the wrinkles around his mouth and eyes. "That, my friend, is my secret."

She twirled a strand of hair. "Wait. I missed something."

"My secret energy source is God."

"Let me check my schedule." What a lame reply. Like she had tons of invitations to choose from. Like she had seriously important projects to complete. Nevaeh fled, feeling pretty much like a rat that no one wanted to see.

As Nevaeh breezed down the city street she realized she couldn't get away from the holiday spirit. Accustomed to seeing others with grimaces and worry-lines scoring their foreheads, or hearing harried moms shouting at their children, or packs of teens roaming the streets without good-will-to-others stamped across their T-shirts, she gaped at the unexpected sights. Last-minute-shopper men, arms brimming with fancy gift bags, stood outside boutiques, as if pondering whether to shop for just one more present. Bakeshops had signs that she ordinarily wouldn't see: Open Late. Sale on Chocolate Yule Logs and Towering Tree Cakes. When Nevaeh rounded the corner, leaving the busy commerce section and entering the residential neighborhood where she lived, she stopped short. A few houses away a handful of carolers sang "Hark The Herald Angels Sing." A man and woman, with their elbows linked, stood beside the open house door and beamed at the singers.

Tears welled in Nevaeh's eyes. As if she were superstitious and had seen a black cat, she crossed the road away from all the merriment.

Why? She wanted to experience that joy too. She wanted family. Friends. She wanted peace.

At the far end of the street she crossed over again to her side. With another few steps she unlocked the door to the outside of her apartment building and when the elevator failed to respond, she raced up the stairs to the fourth floor. Before her door was a wrapped gift with a big red bow and a tin-foiled platter of what she assumed were treats. An envelope rested on top of the latter. With a fingertip she brushed a runaway tear streaking down her cheek and scooped up the surprises.

Inside, seated at the kitchenette's single stool beside the cluttered counter that she used as a table, she began to open the card, guessing it was from Russell. The homemade red and green Christmas card—the only one she'd received this year—was indeed from her next-door neighbor.

Dear Nevaeh. Merry Christmas. May His peace and joy be with you now and always. I hope you enjoy the sweets (I'm only a so-so baker—Ho ho ho.) and may you find the book uplifting. God bless you. From your friend, Russell.

She reached under the tinfoil for a treat, happy to discover a chocolate-covered pretzel rod. As the taste sensation of sweet and salty danced across her tongue, she grabbed the gift-wrapped present she'd set on the counter.

Suddenly, like a child eager to see what Santa brought, she ripped open the wrapping paper with its candy cane theme.

"Oooh," escaped from her lips, though no one was around to hear. *Twelve Christmas Stories For Each Day Of Christmas.*

Okay, okay, she said to herself as she snorted back tears, laughed out loud, and hiccupped. She'd attend church tomorrow evening with her neighbor, after all.

At nine the next evening she rapped on Russell's door. He greeted her with a sparkle of joy lighting his face. "I'm so happy you're going to church with me this Christmas Eve."

"Really? I mean, you look happy . . . you look . . ."

"Like a walking Christmas tree?"

"Well, sort of. I think it's the red pants and green pullover."
She laughed, pressing a finger to her chin. "Am I okay? I'm not
used to going to church. I didn't know what to wear. Maybe I
should change. I'd only be—"

"The skirt and blouse is perfect."

"You sure? I don't look like a cocktail waitress in this black
outfit?"

He waved a hand. "Nah. You're fine."

On their five-block walk to the church, an overwhelming
need to talk fired up Nevaeh.

"Were you born and raised in San Francisco, Russell?"

"Do you really want to hear a sad story tonight?"

"Tell me. I'd enjoy knowing more about you."

"Sometimes I wonder if I relate to the baby Jesus because of
my humble birth. See, I was born in Detroit, but was abandoned
hours afterwards at a police station."

Nevaeh closed the gap between them, and matched his stride.
"That is sad. Was there a happy ending?"

"Absolutely. A couple who prayed and prayed for a baby they
couldn't have adopted me and loved me with all their hearts. We
had a few rough times—like any other family—but I still thank God
daily for the joys He blessed me with. I've learned not to fret over
what I don't have, figuring I do have what He wants me to have."

"That's a different way of looking at things." She thought
about that for a few seconds. "A peaceful way."

"God is peace."

"You and God are pretty close."

"It's the only thing I cling to these days." He pointed to the
street, to the many cars trying to inch into the tight parking spots
before the church. "How about you? Was your family big on the
whole church scene?"

"No way. Mom and Dad never went to church, never talked
about God. I think as a joke they named me what I am."

By the light of the street post she saw him lift a brow. "Nevaeh?"

"Yeah. It's backwards for heaven. And you know what? All my life I've felt backwards, like things are wrong and will stay that way."

Russell pointed to the open church doors. "Nevaeh is a lovely name. You no longer have to feel backwards. With God, you will always move forward."

A sharp pang of contempt twisted within her. "You're not promising a magic wand, are you?"

He flashed a gentle smile. "Something better. Hope."

Before she could ponder a rebuttal or a last second escape, Russell began to climb the steps of the church. And like a child following a parent, Nevaeh hurried after him.

A woman greeted Russell at the inner set of doors. Thinking no one wanted to bother with her, Nevaeh stepped back. *Always backwards, that's what I am.*

The greeter extended a hand to Nevaeh. "Welcome. Any friend of Russell's is a friend of ours. Enjoy the service."

Nevaeh shook the woman's hand, surprised by its warm touch. Actually, she was surprised to find herself in an atmosphere of people exchanging hugs and thumps on the back.

"Want to go in?" Russell asked.

Her words were tangled in the emotions fluttering around her insides. She nodded and began to once again follow Russell. Then she stopped, her feet seemingly glued to the gray carpet. She couldn't stop staring at the sign over the doorway.

"Are you okay, Nevaeh?"

She looked at Russell and then again at the sign hanging above the sanctuary's door. Its carved message stated: Therefore being justified by faith, we have peace with God through our Lord Jesus Christ (Romans 5:1 KJV).

Peace? Nevaeh and peace weren't cozy pals. She often awoke during the dark nights as if fear had morphed into a human form and shook her by her shoulder. Her mind raced during these lonely times. Scary and overwhelming, these thoughts gripped her until the early morning hours, until sleep crept over her for a few minutes before the alarm clock buzzed. Daylight failed to offer her solace. Around others she felt misunderstood. But this peace that God offered? Just the thought of the Supreme Being of all existence, her forever Father who loved her, filled her with tranquility.

Warmth flowed within her, chasing the winter's cold from her bones.

Yeah, she wanted peace. His peace.

Nevaeh looked at her friend. "Yes, I'm fine. And I think I'm going to stay that way."

Together, they walked inside.

About the Author

Elaine Stock never expected that a college major in psychology and sociology would walk her through the see-saw industries of food service and the weight-loss business; co-ownership with her husband in piano restoration; and ten years in community leadership. All great fodder for creating fiction.

In the spring of 2011 Elaine placed in the Semi-finals category in the ACFW Genesis Contest for her novel *Walk With Me*. In 2013 she received the honor of My Book Therapy's Frasier Bronze Medalist award for *No Going Back*. And in 2014 she was blessed with the news that her short story *In His Own Time* won the People's Choice Award in the Family Fiction Contest and will be published in a printed anthology.

Elaine's blog, **Everyone's Story** has been graced by an awesome international viewership. She hosts weekly interviews and reflections from published authors, unpublished writers, and readers who share inspirational stories. Its viewership is dedicated to "Readers, Writers, and All Those In-between."

You can connect with Elaine at:

Website/blog: Everyone's Story: elainestock.com

Twitter: http://www.twitter.com/ElaineStock

Facebook: https://www.facebook.com/AuthorElaineStock

Mary Anne's Gift

DONNA HUBBARD SCOFIELD

JULY, 1859

Henry Hubbard came to church that hot Sunday morning to find a wife. Everybody knew that. The unmarried women hid behind their Bibles while they freed a curl to hang down by an ear, or pinched their cheeks for color. I didn't bother. There were plenty of pretty girls. I was only seventeen, but I already knew I'd be the spinster who stayed on at home and took care of the old folks, and helped out when my brothers' wives had babies. Oh, I didn't have pox scars or a lazy eye or buck teeth, but even the girls who had those problems had something to make up for them... big blue eyes, or thick shiny hair, or a round ripe bosom.

Instead, I had nothing. I was taller than a lot of boys for one thing, and so skinny my bosoms barely made bumps under my shift. Mousy-brown, thin hair wasn't pretty to look at. I had gray-green eyes, like the saddest storm-clouds you'd ever see. My only good feature was clear skin, but I was so shy that anytime anybody looked at me, a blush flared up like bacon grease on a hot fire, and my face and neck turned a blotchy red.

During prayer I peeked under my eyelashes at the back of Henry's head, two pews forward. Blond hair curled around his ears and against his collar, like he needed a wife to take him out in the backyard, tie a cloth around his neck, and give him a trim-ming. His back was rigid as a hickory tree, even though his two little ones were nestled against him. Though he bent his head just enough to look like he was praying, you could tell he really wasn't. The muscles in his neck stood out, and I got the feeling that if he was talking to God, he wasn't thanking Him for blessings.

Henry hadn't been to church since his beautiful wife died five months earlier. Folks said he cursed God at Melissa's death-bed, and you can't get much worse than that. Relatives and friends had cared for little Thomas and Angeline, but he needed a mother for his two young 'uns. Church was the place to find one.

Henry wasn't one of the schoolboys I'd daydreamed about; he was twelve years older. He was tall enough that I wouldn't have to slump my shoulders if I was ever lucky enough to stand beside him…slender, clean-shaven, with deep-set blue eyes and light hair streaked even lighter by the sun. I envied the pretty girl he'd choose to be the new mother for his children.

After the service, he walked over to my stepfather, shook his hand, and said he'd like to court his daughter. Me, Mary Ann Hopkins, the plain one!

That afternoon we walked down the lane. Leaning on the split-rail fence, Henry said, "Mary Ann, I need a wife. I saw you in church today, and I thought to myself, 'now, there's the kind of girl who would be a good mother to my two young 'uns. Somebody modest, and clean and pleasant.'"

I saw the sycamore shade dancing across his handsome face, and felt a pang of pain in my chest. Because my mind was adding the rest of the words to finish what he didn't say: *Somebody who knows how to cook and clean, and make soap and sauerkraut, and be grateful for another woman's children because she never expected to have any of her own. Best of all, somebody who's plain enough to not need courting.*

"Mary Ann, if you're in agreement, I'd like to go back and ask your ma and step-pa for permission to marry you."

And I, of course, said yes.

We got married the following Saturday. It was dusk when Henry carried my little trunk out and put it in his wagon for the trip to my new home. Thomas was asleep, and Angeline almost. A neighbor had offered to keep them overnight, but I knew Henry wanted his young 'uns back home with him, so I'd nudged his arm and whispered, "Thomas and Angeline need to sleep in their own beds again. Can you thank Mrs. Curnutt and tell her no real nicely?"

When we got home we put the children to bed in the little lean-to bedroom downstairs. Henry had put my trunk in the other bedroom, so I went there to unpack it while he did the evening chores. I was sitting in bed, my heart pounding with the uncertainty of what would happen next, when I heard him come in and wash up at the basin by the backdoor.

He came in and sat down on the side of the bed, leaned closer and put his hand on my shoulder. Suddenly a wild sound tore out of his throat, an animal sound almost. I realized it was a sob. He jumped up. "I…I can't," he blurted, backing toward the door. "I'm sorry. I just can't." At the door he said, "I've been sleeping in the loft since…I've been sleeping in the loft. I'll just stay there a while longer, let you get used to things." Then he was gone, scrambling up those loft stairs like a ghost was after him. And maybe there was.

I sat in my new muslin nightgown and heard him climbing the steep stairs. Of course he'd been sleeping in the loft, I thought. This was the bed where he had slept with Melissa, the wife he loved. It was where she'd given birth to their babies. It was where she died.

I changed into my old nightgown, and cried myself to sleep.

Next morning life went on like last night's scene hadn't happened. Angeline came out of the bedroom, dressed and ready to start the day, and her only four years old. "You didn't have to get up so early," I told her. "Breakfast isn't ready yet."

"I can help," she said quickly. "I always helped, when Thomas and I stayed places."

"Did you have to help when your mama was alive?" I asked.

Angeline stared at me. "Well, not much," she replied. "That was Mama."

I realized that the little girl had stayed in homes where she didn't feel quite welcome, and tried to earn a place for herself and her brother. I knelt to her level. "I'm not your mama," I said, "and I'm not going to try to take her place. You'll always love your mama more than anybody. But I'm here to take care of you and Thomas now, and I hope you'll learn to love me, too. And in the meantime…you don't have to earn your keep here." I stood up, and patted the top of her head awkwardly. "You might have to tell me what I need to know to earn *my* keep, though. Does your pa like his gravy thick or thin?"

Angeline grinned at me, the first real smile I'd seen from the child. "I think Pa will like his gravy just fine as long as he doesn't have to make it. He's not a very good cook."

From the doorway Henry boomed, "I heard that, little lady! I'll have you know I'm a good cook. I make the best burned bacon in Cedar Springs!" Angeline giggled and ran across the kitchen to grab him around the knees, and I knew that even if I was the plainest girl in the county, and certainly not pretty enough to go to bed with, I'd done a good thing. I'd brought Henry's two young 'uns back to him.

I knew this wasn't ever going to be some passionate love story from the Bible like Solomon and the Queen of Sheba, and for sure not like David and Bathsheba. Henry would always love Melissa, but he needed a wife. It made me hurt to think of it, so I tried not to. The only time I did much thinking was when I unwrapped my braids from around my head and crawled into bed alone. Then I thought plenty. At the beginning I cried a little, but since I'd gone into the marriage with my eyes open, the crying didn't last long. I knew I was luckier than a lot of girls. Most men married again as soon as they lost a wife; someone had to care for the young 'uns. At least the one I married was clean and decent, and treated me good. After noon dinner he always said, "That was a real good meal, Mary Ann," even if had been only beans and cornbread.

And he only had two young 'uns, not a whole houseful. Getting acquainted with Angeline and Thomas, and keeping up with the work of the house and the farm, kept me too busy for lollygagging.

Angeline was beginning to lose that careful, contained look that a four-year-old shouldn't ever have had, and she smiled more. When her little brother misbehaved, as he often did, Angeline no longer looked at me with a worried expression. Instead, it was with a scornful little smile, like "Well, what can you expect from a baby?" She was sweet, biddable, and helped ease my loneliness more than I ever thought a little girl of only four could do.

Thomas very shortly became Tommy. He wasn't big enough for an old name. Oh, that little tadpole! Not even two years old yet, he was full of the lovable baby antics that made you chuckle even when you wanted to swat him. He'd grab me around the legs, look up at me with those blue, blue eyes so like his pa's, and of course I'd stop what I was doing and pick him up.

When the weather finally began to cool, and the Ozark hills turned gold and orange, we'd been married three months and I was still a maiden, not a wife. I realized that I was beginning to love Henry as much as I did his children. Once I lost a button off my everyday dress and fastened it at the neck with a brooch my granny had given me. Henry said, "You look real pretty today, Mary Ann." I treasured those words for days. I hoped that in the wintertime, snug in the house together, we'd get to know each other better. Maybe by springtime I'd be carrying a little one of my own. In the meantime, I'd enjoy the ones God had loaned me.

I always took the children to church, but Henry didn't go with us. The children and I sat in the Hubbard pew. I remembered when Melissa was alive and Henry was happy, the times he stood in the pulpit and delivered simple sermons when Preacher Ellsworth was sick. He'd been close to God then.

Henry didn't work out in the fields or at the grist mill on the Sabbath, but kept busy with his big mill ledger, writing in his journal, or reading. Often, when we got home, he was reading the Bible. Maybe he didn't hate God, but just couldn't understand Him and was trying to learn how to trust Him again. I didn't know. Of all the mysteries in life, my husband was the greatest.

In early December, Angeline and Tommy were sick – bad sick – with the measles. My ma came over and told me what to do for them. I was too busy right then, but I decided that someday I was going to learn everything I could about herbs and healing.

Henry and I worked together making poultices, spooning fever-few tea, sponging hot little bodies with cool water, changing sheets, and grabbing short naps when the children slept. Once I even woke to find Henry lying beside me, with his arm flung across my hip.

The morning that they were finally on the mend, I threw open the doors and windows to air the smell of sickness and herbs and onion poultices out of the house. I baked fresh bread, and the warm yeasty scent filled the rooms. Angeline and Tommy were able to come to the table for supper. Before anybody lifted a spoon, Henry reached out and took the hand of the child on either side of him. Following his lead, I did the same, until the four of us were connected by joined hands. Bowing his head, Henry said, "Lord, thank You for protecting this family. Bless this food to the nourishment of our bodies. Amen." It was the first time Henry had talked to God since I'd been in his house. It was also the first time I'd really felt like part of his family.

After the children were in bed, my hands went still as Henry bent over me where I was mending and kissed me on the fore-head. When I got ready for bed, I unbraided my hair and brushed it until it made little crackling sparks in the dim light from the open doorway. It looked thicker, from being in braids, and lay in crinkled waves over my shoulders. As I climbed into bed I told myself it didn't really matter if Henry came to me or not…next morning I'd braid my hair neatly again, and put the muslin night-gown back in the chest, and he'd never know I waited for him.

I heard him put his ledger on the shelf, blow out the lamp, and quietly enter the bedroom.

I wanted to hear him say he loved me, but if he couldn't say that, I didn't want to hear anything. He must have sensed my feeling, because he didn't speak. He smoothed the fly-away hair from my face and kissed me very gently. Afterward he whispered, "Now you are my wife, sweet Mary Ann."

I know it was vanity to think about, but in the days to come I wondered sometimes if being with me had helped Henry forgive God for taking Melissa. Maybe he wasn't so lonely. He always said the blessing at mealtime now. And he sat in the little lean-to bedroom and listened while Angeline said her prayers each night. Tommy usually added a few words too, and ended with a loud, vigorous "AY-MEN!" which I could hear even from the kitchen. You could tell that was his favorite part of the prayer. One evening when Henry came out of their room, he said, "When Tommy's a little older, we'll start family prayers in the evenings."

Adding to my happiness that grew day by day, Christmas was coming. I didn't want Angeline's first Christmas without her mama to be empty and sad. She had a rag dolly that she cared for like a real baby, carried around in the crook of her arm, and rocked in Melissa's rocking chair by the fire while she sang to it.

"Her name is Hetty," she confided to me one quiet afternoon. "She's better than a real baby. Hetty doesn't wet her britches or throw little hissy fits to get what she wants, like Tommy does."

During naptime and after the children were in bed at night, I made Hetty dresses exactly like the new ones I had sewed for Angeline that made her so proud. Then I stitched a patchwork quilt from the scraps, to fit the doll cradle Henry had made the previous Christmas, before Melissa died.

It hurt me to think of how warm and happy those Christmases must have been, full of love. I was secure in my place now, but I knew Henry didn't love me as he had Melissa. Whenever those dark thoughts came, I got busier. I made Tommy a soft, cuddly puppy dog out of leftover calico, with button eyes and a red tongue lolling out of its mouth; and I sewed him a stuffed cloth ball to roll back and forth across the floor to Angeline.

When Henry made a trip to Stockton a few days before Christmas, I gathered up the butter I'd stored in the springhouse, and the extra eggs floating in lime water in the cellar.

"Could you trade these for a few sticks of candy for the young 'un's stockings? And if they trade good enough, maybe you could get a few sticks of cinnamon and a nutmeg or two. I want to bake some little cakes for Angeline and Tommy, and the spices in the pantry are about gone."

"Mary Ann, you don't have to use your butter and egg money for the young 'uns' Christmas treats," Henry said, stowing the baskets under the wagon seat. "Save that for something special, something that you want."

"But that's the something special that I want. Lemon sticks and peppermint sticks, and spices for cakes."

A few days before Christmas, Henry put a little cedar tree in a bucket of sand by the kitchen window, and the children and I had fun hanging trimmings on it. Henry went out to the barn until we were finished, so I knew he was remembering Christmases with Melissa.

On Christmas Eve the children hung their stockings by the fireplace, and after they were asleep I baked a pan of spiced honey cake and cut it in little squares. Henry brought in from the barn the play table and two stools he'd made for Angeline and Tommy. We filled their stockings with the stick candy, honey cakes, an apple and some hickory nuts, and arranged the gifts we had made on the hearth below the stockings.

When Henry and I went to bed he pulled me into his arms and was very slow and gentle. Ma was wrong. This wasn't just a woman's duty to put up with.

Next morning Angeline and Tommy were so excited about their gifts and stockings that I thought my heart was going to burst with pride. I let them eat two little honey cakes and have a few licks of their candy sticks after breakfast, then put the treats up on the mantel to get ready for church.

Henry came down from the loft with a soft package wrapped in brown store-keeper's paper and handed it to me awkwardly. "I know you'll like what's in the middle," he said. "I'm not so sure about what's wrapped around it."

Why, he *had* noticed me reading and re-reading the few books on the shelf by his ledger. The gift on the very inside was a book by an English woman named Jane Austen. Those crisp new pages and that ink-and-leather book smell made me want to forget all about church, sit down and read, but I had to be satisfied to stroke it, smell it, and murmur, "Oh, thank you, Henry, thank you." Then I unfolded what it had been wrapped in, that had made the package soft. It was a shawl, knit so loosely that it looked almost like lace. It was a dark rose color. I draped it over my head and let it hang off my shoulders.

Henry nodded his head knowingly. "Go look in the mirror," he said. I did, and saw that the color made my hair look darker and my cheeks pinker, and my gray-green eyes were sparkling. Oh, my! Mary Ann Hopkins Hubbard, the plain one, looked almost pretty!

I couldn't decide which was the best Christmas present: the book, or the shawl, or Angeline's joyful cry of "Oh, thank you, Mama!" when she saw the dolly dresses I'd sewed. A short while later I knew what the best gift was: sitting in the Hubbard pew as a family on Christmas morning, hearing that beautiful old story with Henry beside me, Tommy on my lap, Angeline nestled between us. That was the gift that would bless me all my life.

About the Author

Donna Hubbard Scofield has been writing a Yakima Herald column "The Family Chuckle" for twelve years. She began writing in earnest upon retirement from the Yakima School District after twenty-eight years as an elementary school office manager and administration building secretary.

She bought her first computer with earnings from women's confession magazines...yes, those "true" stories. That portion of her career ended when her devoutly religious mother found out about the story titled "Mama Loved Us, But She Loved the Bottle More."

A novella was published by Harlequin/Silhouette under the pseudonym Lynn Russell (her middle name and her husband's first name). She has had short stories published in women's magazines, and was fourth place winner in the national short story contest held by Country Woman. She is the author of two books, The Family Chuckle (selections from her first ten years of columns) and Back Home, historical fiction. Publisher Lighthouse of the Carolinas is preparing her most recent book, That First Montana Year, for publication in August, 2015.

Donna and her husband live in Yakima, Washington and raised their four children there. When not writing, she enjoys doing research for her books, and traveling to their sites. She loves writing, and whenever possible she whips out stories for her six-year old grandson and two great-great-grandsons, age three-and-a-half and fifteen months. She is grateful to God for the blessings He has given her in this life.

You can find her online at her Facebook page: https://www.facebook.com/pages/Donna-Hubbard-Scofield-Author-Page/113918238798943?ref=bookmarks

Special Assignment

KATHLEEN ROUSER

"Yes, at least we know another drug pusher will have a merry Christmas!" Lucy Meriwether slammed the phone down. That judge had no business posting such a small bail for the first offense low-life, even if it was Christmas Eve. She rubbed her pounding temples and surveyed the pile of unfinished reports on her desk.

Lucy stood and stuffed several pieces of paperwork into her messenger bag. Before turning to go, she moved toward the window. Colorful blinking Christmas lights up and down Main Street taunted her. Arms crossed, she leaned forward, resting her forehead against the cool pane. Sparkling snowflakes piled on the outside ledge. She hated the holidays.

"Detective Meriwether?" A singsong voice with a Scottish burr pierced the silence.

Lucy grazed the pocket of her blazer, where her gun rested underneath, secure in its holster. She looked at the reflection in the window—a rather heavyset woman held a little boy's hand.

"Who wants to know?" She turned toward them and crossed her arms again.

"I'm Florence Murgatroyd from Child Protection Services. This wee bairn was abandoned on the street. Do you investigate such things here?"

"Child *Protective* Services?"

"Aye, but I'm here on temporary assignment." Florence pushed her round wire-rimmed glasses, which looked vintage, up the bridge of her nose. "Seems they need extra help this time of year."

"I'm leaving. This isn't really my area of investigation." Lucy waved a hand toward the hallway. The forlorn child beside Florence wiped his runny nose on his dirty sleeve. Yuck. She latched the flap on her bag. "Not much I can do right now anyway. What about social services?"

Florence cleared her throat. "They're closed for the holiday and all the foster families are full up. I can't find anyone to take little Jacob here. Where's he going to spend Christmas?"

"What about with you, Mrs. Murgatroyd?" Lucy studied the hefty woman with an ample lap for children. Kindness was written in her soft brown eyes. Graying curls framed her face.

"Ach, no! It's just me and me elderly mum. He needs to be with younger people, perhaps a family."

"Well, I don't—"

"Nonsense! All he has in the world is in this bag." She pushed it toward Lucy. "We'll find a placement for him in a couple of days."

Before Lucy knew it, she held Jacob's hand and the rumpled grocery bag while Mrs. Murgatroyd was heading toward the door. "Be good for Miss Lucy now. Merry Christmas, loves."

The child's dark hair stood up on end and dirt streaked across his nose and cheeks, underneath bright gray eyes. Jacob couldn't have been more than six years old. *This is highly irregular!* Her stomach knotted, but she couldn't leave him here.

She trembled at this new responsibility. Jacob shook too. After all, she was a stranger. "Come along, Jacob, it's time to go."

The little guy nodded.

Lucy shivered as they walked toward the parking lot. The swirling bits of lace grew into the blizzard predicted earlier. When they reached her black Kia Soul, she buckled Jacob in. He wiggled a bit. "You'll need to sit still now." Lucy used her firmest tone and the child stiffened. She squeezed Jacob's rough, chapped hand, not wanting to frighten him, just make him obey. Lucy was used to hunting down criminals, not playing in the church nursery.

Jacob's teeth chattered. He wasn't wearing a very heavy jacket. She reached into the back for a blanket to drape over the front of him. "Here you go. Keep your hands underneath."

The windshield wipers swished through the snow on the front window. Lucy turned the heat to high and grabbed a brush to clean the rest of the car off. By the time they pulled onto Main Street, the snowstorm obstructed her view. This was just great. What was she going to do for Christmas with a little kid she didn't know? In a blizzard? Preferring to be alone, Lucy had tried to explain to Mrs. Murgatroyd that she didn't have any family nearby.

Christmas was like any other day, except worse. Three years before, her fiancé, Troy, had left her at the altar, right before their perfect Christmas Eve wedding was to begin.

Troy had said she placed too much importance on her job. Besides, she hadn't been sure about having kids. She didn't have that pie-in-the-sky idea about family. Was it her fault she had to help raise her younger brother and sister after her father left her mom?

Jacob sniffled. The kid hadn't asked for this either. He reminded her of her brother when he was little. Lucy's heart thawed just a bit, unlike the weather outside.

She turned the radio on and then off again when all she could find was corny Christmas music or heavy metal blaring through the speakers. Lucy slowly accelerated, trying to steer straight.

"Miss Lucy, are you an angel?"

"What?" *Are you kidding? Definitely not! I'm just a grumpy woman trying to avoid the holidays.* Lucy shrugged against the itchy wool scarf around her neck.

"After Mommy died, Chad said that she was in heaven asking God to send an angel to watch over me."

"Chad?"

"Mommy's boyfriend."

Lucy swallowed against the lump in her throat. "What about your daddy? Where's he?"

"Don't know."

Lucy gritted her teeth, wishing she could get a hold of both men and give them a good thrashing. Jacob was expressionless at declaring this cold, hard fact of life. Well, that's one thing they had in common . . . deadbeat dads. Another layer of defense melted away like ice on a flaming barbecue.

When she looked back at the road, colorful clothing flashed past as someone ran out in front of her. The car swerved hard into the curb as Lucy pumped the breaks. Pow! The explosive popping made her jump. She turned on her hazard lights. Shifting the car to park and jumping out, she hoped to see, despite the heavy snow, whether someone had been hurt.

"Stay put, Jacob." Lucy trudged toward the front of the car. There was no sign of anyone injured lying in the road. She exhaled. "Thank you, God."

Remembering the explosion, she held onto the front hood as she made her way to the curbside of the car. The front tire was as flat as sliced cheese. Could the day get any worse? Jacob watched her through the window, looking like some waif in a Dickens' novel.

Lucy got back into the car and punched in the number for her favorite garage only to have the phone shut down. Hadn't the cell battery been charged the night before? She reached over and opened the glove compartment.

"Looking for somethin'?"

"Yes, my phone's car charger." Lucy felt around in the dark and grabbed her flashlight, but even when she shined it inside the glove compartment, she didn't find the cord.

"Can I see the flashlight?" For the first time Jacob smiled at her.

"Sure." Lucy placed it in his hand. She pushed her long dark hair off her face, combing her fingers over the top of her head. *Now what do I do? I can't make Jacob walk two miles back to the apartment in this. Please, God, help me figure this out!* Closing her eyes for a minute, the headache returned.

Bang! Bang! The pounding on the window might as well be in her head. Lucy's eyes popped open. "Are you all right in there?"

Lucy didn't want to scare Jacob by revealing her Glock, but she didn't trust anyone out there. Until . . . a larger flashlight shone into the car and a familiar voice registered. "Lucy? Lucy Meriwether? Is that you in there?"

She popped out her side of the car. "Ben Fremont? What are you doing here?"

"Just moved back from Denver. Staying with my mom until I find a place. I heard your tire blow and saw the lights flashing. Thought I'd see who might need help."

"Amanda here too?" She figured he'd be married to his high school sweetheart by now.

"We were engaged, but she had second thoughts. Wanted to meet other people." The dimple she'd always thought was so cute appeared with his ironic smile. Blond curls pushed out from under his hat, shimmering with snowflakes. Under the streetlight, he was still the same hunky guy who'd been off limits during their high school years. "Why don't you and your son come in and warm up until you can get a hold of your husband."

Lucy threw her head back in laughter and couldn't stop until she had to wipe the tears from her cheeks before they froze. She could imagine how the situation must look to him.

"What?" Ben shrugged.

"I'll explain. Come on, Jacob." She ducked into the car and unbuckled him, lifting him into her arms since he wasn't wearing any boots. The boy wasn't very heavy for his size. He clung to the paper bag in one hand and flashlight in the other. Ben escorted them into the red brick colonial, as warm and inviting on the inside as it was on the outside.

Mrs. Fremont was hanging ornaments on the Christmas tree in front of the picture window. "Lucy Meriwether? How are you? It's been much too long."

Lucy had forgotten how kind the Fremonts were. She shrugged out of her coat and introduced them to Jacob, and her predicament. Ben's mother took Jacob to the kitchen for hot chocolate and cookies. Lucy and Ben fell into easy conversation as though they'd never lost contact. Her face heated as she shared about being left at the altar by Troy, but when Ben's gray eyes warmed with understanding, the connection to him was worth it.

"Would you like something hot to drink?" Ben leaned forward and touched her hand. The warm electricity coursing up her arm took her breath for a moment.

"Sure. I'd love some hot chocolate." *To soothe my nerves.* Another layer of defense peeled away. It was nice to be a welcomed guest and not an interfering detective for a few minutes.

Jacob ran toward her with a smile on his face. The streaks of dirt were gone, no doubt due to Mrs. Fremont's help, and his hair smoothed down. She'd make a wonderful grandma.

"Miss Lucy, can we stay here for Christmas?" He grabbed onto her arm and leaned his head on her shoulder.

"Lucy, I insist you and this darling little boy stay for dinner tonight. It's getting late." Mrs. Fremont stood with hands on her hips.

"Well, I—"

"We'd love to have you help decorate the tree, too. It's a nasty storm out there and every garage will be closed by now. Besides, we haven't finished catching up." Ben handed her a steaming mug.

"Ple-e-ease." Jacob put on a puppy face.

"Well, all right then." Lucy nodded.

"Yay!" Jacob clapped his hands together. He ran to retrieve his paper bag, left by the front door. "I got a present from Mrs. Murgatroyd. Can I open it now?"

Lucy looked to Ben, not wanting to upset their Christmas traditions. "Sure, tiger, go ahead." He winked at Jacob, just as delighted at the prospect.

"Ben, have you seen our treetop angel around?" Mrs. Fremont dug through a box of decorations. "I was sure it was right here."

"No, I haven't." He shrugged and turned to watch Jacob pull the bright green paper from a square box, then the lid.

"An angel!" Jacob pulled it out. "Mrs. Murgatroyd told me it was something special for a Christmas tree!"

"Well, what do you know?" Ben scratched his chin. "I think we have a new one, Mom."

A rotund angel with gray curls and wire-rimmed spectacles, with one eye winking. It looked more like a fairy godmother with its calico skirt and silver wings. But other than the long skirt and wings, she looked awfully familiar. *Mrs. Murgatroyd?*

Jacob showed the treetop angel to Ben, who stood and led the child to the tree, sharing his joy. Lucy sipped hot cocoa, watching the two with wonder as Ben lifted the little one so he could place his gift atop the tree. They looked right together.

"Come have a closer look at our handiwork." Ben came and took her hand, sending her temperature up with his captivating smile. Jacob giggled and squeezed in between them. For the first time in several years, Lucy belonged. Maybe getting married and having a family was worth the risk. In fact, it surprised her that such a thought seemed suddenly downright perfect.

About the Author

Kathleen Rouser has loved making up stories since she was a little girl. Her debut novella, *The Pocket Watch,* is part of *Brave New Century,* a Christian historical romance anthology, published in 2013 by Prism Book Group (Inspired Romance). Kathleen has also been published in *Homeschool Digest* and An *Encouraging Word* magazines and the *Oakland Press.* She contributes regularly to Novel PASTimes, a blog devoted to promoting mainly Christian historical fiction. She is a long time member in good standing of ACFW and a former board member of its Great Lakes Chapter.

A former homeschool instructor, Kathleen continues to teach children through the ministry of Community Bible Study. She lives in Michigan with her hero and husband of 33 years, Jack, who not only listens to her stories, but also cooks for her.

Find her at:

Website - www.kathleenrouser.com

Facebook - https://www.facebook.com/kerouser

Facebook Author Page - https://www.facebook.com/kathleenerouser

Twitter - @KathleenRouser - https://twitter.com/KathleenRouser

Pinterest - https://www.pinterest.com/kerouser/

the Quilt

Wake Up

and

Under the tree

KARLENE JACOBSEN

the Quilt

Snowflakes chased each other to the ground, snatching for themselves parcels of earth as others lighted next to them, creating a brilliant white blanket speckled with diamonds and crystals that winked at the sky when the moon peeked through the clouds. I leaned against the window's frame, gazing through the pane, awed by the peaceful invasion of these tiny visitors from the heavens above. The glass, cold against my forehead, contrasted the orange, red, and gold flickering of the flames in the fireplace across the room. By the reflection in the windowpane, I could see the fire embrace the logs as its tongues licked and lapped the bark.

A twinge of guilt tried to cloud my euphoria. I pressed it down, determined not to allow my husband's absence to bother me. For years, we had gotten caught up in the frenzy of shopping, baking, parties – all the trimmings that accompanied a *happy* holiday season. In November and December we drove the credit cards to their limits, and then the next ten months we worked feverishly to pay them off, just in time to begin shopping again. Then one day, I had a *revelation* about Christmas. It's a pagan holiday, as my dad always told me. We shouldn't be celebrating it; in fact, all Christians ought to boycott Christmas. My husband and I are united on one point – we don't know exactly when Christ was born. The rest, he staunchly disagrees with me, ergo his absence when the cabin is so cozy and inviting.

We argued again. He invited me along to take gifts to the homeless shelters. "There are thousands this year who have no home, let alone the ability to celebrate Christmas. We've been blessed beyond measure. Why don't we do this for them?"

"Because, Jeremy, it's wrong." I slapped the back of one hand into the palm of the other. "Can't you see . . . we shouldn't be celebrating a pagan holiday; we need to dispense with them and celebrate the feasts."

I turned my gaze from the flickering lights in the window to the blaze wrapping its arms around the logs. *Doesn't it bother You that it's not really Your Holy Day? Shouldn't we be bothered as well?* My fingers traced the squares of the quilt I draped around my shoulders, lingering on each of the pieces of fabric Grandma had pointed out. I could almost see her crooked fingers shake as she traced the patterns on the gingham, explaining, *"You see, Dana, quilts we made when I was young told stories. They were stories of love and loss, celebrations and mourning. Every one of them is woven into this quilt."*

"Tell me the story, Grandma." Her stories captivated me. Each square represented a different story. She caressed blue denim squares that looked to be smeared with ink and explained how Great Grandpa—her daddy—wore the same shirt every day to work. Great Grandma would wash it at night and have it ready for him in the morning.

"It was his favorite – his lucky shirt – he said." Grandma had laughed, gently stroking the pieces, *"Of course, he thought it so."* Grandma's eyes caught a wistful glow. *"Mama used to laugh whenever she told me why he refused to throw it away even when it grew more holes than it was designed to have. It was the shirt he wore the day he married her."* For hours, Grandma talked of the pieces of fabric, telling the stories each piece held. I learned about my mom's first date, her first prom, and the first time Uncle Henry broke his leg and had to have his Sunday best pants ripped open.

Oh, I wish I had stories like that to tell. I left my place at the window and settled into the red and gold striped sofa facing the fireplace. My face captured the warmth as the flames licked the opening that led to the chimney. Caught in the memories that marched across my heart, I lost track of time and space.

The snap, crackle, pop, and sizzle from the logs startled me. Until then, I hadn't realized that my head bobbed.

My mind drifted back to the argument Jeremy and I had before he left with the kids. I scanned the walls, noting the pictures of lighthouses and oceans hung above Scripture verses. Then I thought about the quilt. "If *You* had a quilt, what story would it tell?" I tried to imagine what pieces of fabric God would insert into the masterpiece He'd create, knowing each square would represent something dear to Him.

Of course, there was no answer. What did I expect? Booming voices? Thunder? Lightning? Yeah, right. God doesn't speak like He did in the Old Testament. I pulled my feet into the quilt and scooted myself down so that I could lay my head on the armrest and watch the fire. Before long, the drugging effects of sleep overtook me as my body melted into the cushions of the sofa. My eyes closed. I could still see the flickering light of the fire glowing bright hues of red behind my lids. Then it faded.

For how long it was dark, I cannot tell. However, the lights reappeared, brighter and more magnificent than before. I stood in the midst of a large room, and although the sunlight beamed in each window, shadows were nonexistent. The furniture, ornately carved, lined in gold, silver and jewels I'd never seen or heard of glimmered in the light pouring in through each crystal clear pane. How they had the clarity they did while shimmering with lights found in diamonds I'll never understand, but they were. I willed my feet to whisper as I walked across the marbled floor to peer out into the lush gardens surrounding the place. Upon closer examination, there were intricately designed images etched in the glass that acted as prisms, casting rainbows both inside and out.

A rustle from behind caught my attention and I turned to see what, or who, approached. Before me stood a man, more magnificent than any I'd ever seen. His height, immeasurable. His hair, like snow. His eyes, blazing like fire.

I wobbled in his presence. The sense that I should be on my knees—probably on my face—filled my pounding heart. I couldn't speak, but wanted to ask, "Who are you?"

"You want to know about my quilt?" He moved toward the window near me and opened a chest. A large quilt lay folded inside. I followed Him to a sofa in the center of the room. "Here, sit, and I will show you." Together, we sat on a bench built to the side of a large hall where a throne could be seen at the end. His actions, so like Grandma's as his hands caressed the fabric. I marveled at His gentleness, both with me and with the obvious antique in His lap.

"This." His fingers smoothed a square that appeared to be cut from royal garments. "This is taken from the fabric worn by the King before the promised gift appeared to man." His eyes moistened. The pleasure and, dare I say pride, in His voice swelled as He told me of the day the King, His Son, walked away from His throne. "He and I spoke often of that day. Then one day He rose from His throne, slipped out of His sandals, laid His crown on the cushion, and shrugged out of His royal robes. Although He knew many wouldn't recognize Him, some would reject Him, and others would abuse Him, He remained true to the plan. 'It is important that I go. Without My gift, they will forever be searching and rarely finding freedom.'" He then traced the torn shreds of another square—scarlet in color. His tears soaked into the quilt. "This is the robe they put on His back the day He finished His work."

From beginning to end, the Man shared the story of the King's passionate love for His kingdom. So powerful that He gave His life for them, fully aware many would reject His offer.

Mesmerized by the story of how the Master of the Universe stripped Himself of glory and napped in a bed of hay, I wept. "It's so beautiful. I almost forgot."

He pulled me into His embrace, lavishing kisses on my cheek. "It's all right. Many do. What is important is that you remember why the King appeared to mankind."

I closed my eyes and snuggled into His chest and embraced the warmth that radiated from His being. When I opened them again to look into His face, I found myself back in the cabin's family room facing the dying embers of the fire. I rubbed my eyes in wonder and a bit confused. Had I fallen asleep? I couldn't remember.

To the right of the fireplace, sat a package left by my husband. Unwinding my legs from the quilt, I made my way to the package and untied the bow immaculately arranged and affixed on top. Inside the flap was a card, my husband's bold handwriting smiling up at me. I opened it and read: *"It matters little when, but HOW we remember the greatest gift ever given."*

The box was filled with tissue, which found its way to the floor or into the dying fire, giving it life again. At the bottom was a doll, wrapped in a blanket—swaddled actually—and holding its thumb in its mouth. A note attached read: "The greatest gifts come in tiny packages. We may never realize how they impact us until we nurture them and watch them grow."

Wake Up

I lay there, on my stomach, blankets pulled securely over my head. Determination and procrastination were invited to keep me company. My eyes were glued shut, hoping to block any stray ray of light that found its way under the blankets.

Maybe I can hide here all day.

The sounds of my door creaking open and feet pattering across the floor, along with giggles and warnings to "Shhhhhhh…," filtered in through my barricade against the day.

Someone was on the bed next to me. Blankets moved and before long the warm body of my four-year old, Ellie, slid in. She snuggled up to my side, just like every morning.

A smile crept in with her, etching itself on my face. Then an arm planted itself across my back. The body attached could be none other than Jason, my eight year old.

I chanced a peak through a porthole I made between the blankets and pillows. There he was, staring back at me. If the corners of his mouth could, I'm sure they would've curled around his ears.

"It's Christmas, Mom." Jason rolled his eyes. I should've known better. "Get up." He had more important things to do than to spend time using many words.

"Yeah, Mommy. I want presents!" Ellie bounced out from under the covers.

"Where's Daddy?" I know I sounded like a whiner at that moment, and I'd probably apologize for it later. But sometimes, being a mom is so hard. Didn't anyone understand that I'd only been in bed two hours?

"Downstairs—" Jason scowled at his sister when she interrupted him.

"He said we can't have presents 'til you're up!" Ellie continued to bounce on the bed, rattling my full bladder.

"Ellie. Jason." John stood in the doorway. "Leave your mother alone. She hardly slept last night." I could tell he worked hard to look stern, but the crinkles in the corners of his eyes spoke an entirely different story. When it came to surprises, he was worse than the children.

He shooed Jason and Ellie from the room. Their chins drooped close to their chests as they muttered something about presents and food. There would be no relief if I knew John and that errant look of his.

John sat on the bed next to me. "So. When're you getting up?" Was that a whine I heard in his voice?

"I thought you said I could sleep." Only I was licensed to whine, after spending the night wrapping and cooking and cleaning.

"I did let you sleep. It's nearly six-thirty." He laughed then hopped off the bed. "Come on. I want presents." When I didn't move, he turned, planted his hands on the bed and frowned at me. Those eyes of his give him away every time. I knew it was a pitiful attempt at being offended by my sluggish behavior. It took all my strength to keep from laughing at him.

I sat up, rubbed the sleep from my eyes, ready for the coffee I smelled. He must have somehow instructed the kids to get the pot brewing. "Okay, what are you up to?"

Like a kid let loose in a toy store, he bounded from the bed and flew about the room gathering jeans, sweatshirt, socks and anything else I might need to wear and threw them on the bed. "Come on, get dressed. I've got coffee started." Then he was out the door.

The door clicked shut and his footsteps pounded down the steps before I could ask any further questions.

I dressed, brushed my hair and teeth, and then found my way to the kitchen. The scene I walked into was out of a dream. The only parts of my body that weren't paralyzed by shock were my hands. They flew to my face, at first hiding the tears, then to rub my eyes of any sleep residue, certain I was seeing things. I really needed to wake up.

I hadn't seen my brother, Alex, in four years .since he'd left for Afghanistan with the Marines, and there he was, seated at my table, with a grin that could touch New York and London with each corner of his mouth. No one dared hope he might be home in time for Christmas. But there he was, drinking *my* coffee in *my* kitchen.

Tears crested his eyes. "Merry Christmas, sis." His voice cracked as he unfolded his bulky frame from the chair. Had he wondered whether he would make it home also? I was soon enveloped in one of his famous bear hugs. If this were merely a dream, I didn't want to wake. I prayed I wouldn't wake.

The complaints of my children broke through our moment. "Can we open our presents now?"

"Were we this impatient?" Alex and I separated, both our faces wet with the tears we'd shed. I noted the spot on his uniform where I'd soaked it. A trivial thing compared to his safety.

"Do Mom and Dad know you're here?" I'd nearly forgotten them in my shocked amazement.

He chuckled, "Yep. I woke them promptly at five this morning with breakfast in bed. They're on their way over. It was quite the feat to get over here and see you before them." He bent over and lifted Ellie into his arms and carried her to the tree in the family room. To watch the spark in his eyes dance with the mischief I remembered from childhood made it seem as though time reversed for a moment.

John and I were left alone in the kitchen. He leaned against the counter next to the coffee pot, his gaze intent on me. As I walked toward him, he held out my coffee mug, but I dismissed it and threw my arms around his neck. "Thank you for getting me out of bed."

"Any time." Arm in arm, we made our way to the family room.

Under the Tree

The gifts were wrapped and placed carefully under the tree. My tired bones ached and begged for me to allow them a respite from all the preparations of the season.

My husband had implored me to come to bed hours ago, but he had to know I just could not. "It's for the children." I reasoned. "Christmas is for the children."

He sighed wearily as he turned and trudged up the stairs to our room. I waited silently as his heavy footsteps slowed and softened until at last there was nothing. He was in bed. I resented him for that; apparently he just did not understand what Christmas was all about.

One day, our children will be grown and gone with their own families. Christmas will be over for us. You'll see... I promised the chair that once occupied my husband as though he were still there listening.

I feverishly went about baking cookies for Santa, wrapped every present in shiny silver, red and gold, followed by intricate bows on each package. I made sure the candies, ambrosia salad, and pistachio pudding were made. The kids just loved those and their colors were so festive. The ham and turkey were dressed and ready to go in the oven come morning.

Pride filled my heart. I scanned the room before turning out the lights. *The children will be so happy when they see all that I've done.*

*Dan will be sorry one day that he was not here helping more. I just know
he will.*

The stairs mocked me when I pondered the climb. Deciding
against it, I turned to where the recliner welcomed me with open
arms. I fell into it gratefully and allowed my eyelids their rule as
they sealed shut for a much needed midnight nap.

"You don't remember, do you , Sarah?"

"What? Who are you? What do you mean?"

"Sarah, I miss you."

"How can you miss me? I don't even know you." I searched about,
seeing no one. The voice was familiar, but I was sure we'd never met.

"I'm over here, Sarah…" I followed the voice. I searched and searched.
Becoming frustrated, I decided to give up and go back to bed. *"Sarah, I
miss you."*

My eyes fell on the nativity beneath the tree. There they were, that
little family, the wise men, the shepherds, and all those little animals, all
present and accounted for. My gaze moved from them to the figure of a
man standing just beyond a cross. Was He crying?

I knelt down to get a closer look. *"Sarah, I miss you,"* He said.

"I don't understand.. I'm right here…" I began, then realized I had
been preoccupied with activity and forgot about Him. I began to weep.
"I'm sorry, I've missed You too. Please forgive me."

"Mommy, what are you doing?" Tommy, my six year old,
stood over me, hands on his hips.

I ran a hand through my hair, rubbed my eyes and struggled
to sit up. "Why?"

"You were sleeping under the tree!" His tone took on that of
a prosecuting attorney.

I glanced around, trying to get my bearings straight. Apparently
he was right. "I don't know how I got here," I confessed.

"Mommy loves Jesus!" My two-year old girl bounced, sending
her springy golden hair flying about her face, her arm outstretched

with a forefinger pointing at my hand where I clenched the figure of Jesus.

"Yes I do. And do you know why?" Fully awake now, I realized why I was snuggled with the gifts beneath the tree.

"Why?" I heard Dan louder than the children.

"Well, it was because of Him that we celebrate Christmas. He came to earth to redeem us from sin and give us life. No one really knows what day He was born, so we celebrate on this day. His birth isn't the end of the story. Would you like to hear all of it?"

"YEAH!" I fought the urge to cover my ears and protect them from the shouts. Dan brought over his Bible and read the story from Luke that told of Jesus' death and resurrection.

He finished, closed his Bible and looked over at me, eyes reddened and filled with moisture. "So, is Christmas still for the children?"

"No, it's for all of us." I walked over and wrapped my arms around his neck and was enveloped in his embrace. "Thank you for your patience." I'd been given many priceless gifts in my life. It was time I slowed down and cherished them. Dan and I settled into his recliner and watched the children tear through their presents.

About the Author

Everyone has a dream. Some have a fistful. Karlene Jacobsen falls in the middle. She's been married for twenty-four years, has four amazing children and a Border collie/Australian cattle dog. While she's living out this part of her dream, she is pursuing two others: writing and nursing.

She describes her writing as *sandbox time*. Although she hopes her work will encourage and entertain others, she finds great joy and fulfillment in expressing her heart on paper through story, fiction and nonfiction. Several of her short stories have been published with Christian Fiction Online Magazine, Faith Writers, and her own website; and nonfiction has made its appearance on Jewels of Encouragement and The Barn Door.

Karlene's website: www.karlsajac.blogspot.com

Jewels of Encouragement: www.jewelsofencouragement.com

The Barn Door: www.thebarndoor.net

Faith Writers' profile: http://www.faithwriters.com/member-profile.php?id=35871

His Eye is on the Sparrow

SUSAN F. CRAFT

$\mathcal{E}$leanor Stevens stopped at the end of the checkout counter to loop her grocery bag around her wrist. The weight from the three cans of soup dug the plastic handles into her skin.

I guess you could call it skin, she thought, studying the parchment-thin flesh that no longer hid the blue lines pulsating beneath the surface.

She wriggled the crook of her cane out of the rungs on the back of the grocery cart. Her trusty cane, dubbed *Boaz*, whose Biblical name means *nimble*, wasn't vital for Eleanor, who used him only occasionally when the niggling vertigo attacked or when her pacemaker kicked in. Consequently, she had a tendency to lose track of the walking stick, especially at church. If asked, she preferred leaning on the arms offered by the inevitable corps of gallants who stood ready to serve as escorts.

On those occasions, she would drape her arm through theirs and say, "How very kind of you," in a voice still soft and sweet as the outside petal of a magnolia blossom before it detaches and falls to the ground. She would flash one of her smiles, flutter her eyelashes, and gaze at them with her hazel eyes made even more green in contrast with her gardenia-white hair.

As she draped the hook of *Boaz* across her arm, she noticed that the mailing label glued to the light-pine wood buckled on one side. *I'll have to fix that.* She had misplaced the cane many times in the past year, and the label, with her name and address, had led its finders to her doorstep.

With the bag dangling from one arm and the cane on the other, she pushed the empty buggy away from the counter, passing a row of three-foot-tall, blow-up Christmas trees. A rendition of

"The Twelve Days of Christmas," sung in a fashion suitable more to a lounge lizard, blared over the loud speakers. Eleanor cringed, unsure which offended her most, the trees or the music.

"Let me get that for you, Mizz Stevens" said the store manager, who hurried toward her. The tail of his lighted elf hat jingled with each step.

"No thank you, Jason. I'm fine. It's just soup."

Just soup, she mused on her way out the door. *That's all I've been living off of for months. Don't seem to have an appetite anymore.*

She tottered toward her car, parked in the handicapped space closest to the store entrance.

The first among her group of friends to apply for a handicapped sticker, she'd taken criticism from those who had dug their heels into the playground of life and who planned to go only kicking and screaming into senior citizenship.

"Why not?" she would ask, countering their protests. "If I've learned one thing in my seventy-plus lifetime it's this. If you need a hearing aid, get one. If you need a handicapped sticker, get one. If you can get things on discount Wednesdays, get them."

When she reached her car, a robin's-egg blue 1986 Chevrolet Caprice she had christened *Asher*, she placed her cane on the trunk. *Asher's* name came from the eighth son of Jacob who had been promised shoes of iron and brass, endurance and longevity. *Asher* had served her well for more than seventeen years.

Searching her handbag for keys, she frowned when she couldn't find them. After plopping the groceries on top of the car, she patted the sides of her coat. Hearing the familiar jingle, she reached in the pocket and pulled out the keys.

I probably ought to hang them around my neck, she thought, unlocking the door. In her mind she saw dangling along with the keys, her reading glasses, the favorite pen she used to write countless lists of to-dos, and the long-handled wooden backscratcher that seemed to be forever getting lost in the bedcovers.

She retrieved her grocery bag and shoved it across the front seat. With a groan, she slid behind the steering wheel and closed the door. As she drove away, she wrinkled her brow wondering if she'd forgotten something. *Saltines?*

There were several more errands to run before she finally made her way home. It wasn't until several hours later that she realized she could not find *Boaz*.

"Where in the world did I leave him this time?"

Settling down in the Laura Ashley pink and green striped chair, she gazed out the bay window at her azalea garden. The cozy nook where she spent her quiet time every morning usually held a live Christmas tree, but this year, she had settled for a ceramic tabletop tree purchased from an antique store. Plugged in, the tree's miniature bulbs shone so dim they needed a lighted match to see them. After pondering a while, she couldn't remember the last time she used her cane.

She picked up the phone and dialed the number of her best friend Isabel Ravenel.

"Well, I've lost it again," she said in response to Isabel's greeting.

"Your mind or your tempah," Isabel spoke in her Low Country Charleston, South Carolina drawl – an accent born of 300-year-old-family money, elongated by the Gullah dialect of former slaves who inhabited the sea islands, tempered by the stubborn pride of stiff-necked Secessionists, and softened by the whispers of Spanish-moss shawls draping from live oak trees.

"My cane, you ninny."

"I decla'ah. Why do you insist on carryin' that thing around? It's most unattractive."

"I don't care a fig for the way it looks. And besides, it would be much more unattractive to find oneself sprawled flat on the front lawn of the church."

"Well, I'm fixing to call the prayah line. Would you like us to pray for you?"

"Don't you even think of it!"

"Whyever not? A little prayah goes a long way."

"That may perfectly well be true, but I'm uncomfortable about going to the Lord for such a trivial request."

"Not at all. Remembah, His eye is on the sparrah."

"Well … That's true."

"Try it. It certainly couldn't hurt. Oh, my, I've got to run. Good luck in findin' your cane, Sugah. See you in church tomorrah?

"Yes. I'll be there."

Eleanor hung up and, thinking about Isabel's advice, she opened her Bible where she had left off that morning, in the book of Luke before the passage about God's love for sinners. The first word she read was *lost*. Astounded, she offered up a prayer for assistance for her predicament, for strength to walk about without her cane, and for the attacks of vertigo to cease until she could find it.

A moment after she whispered, "Amen," the doorbell rang. When she opened the front door, she was surprised to find the mailman, Henry Ackerman. *Thank heaven, it's cold enough for him to wear his long pants.* His knobby knees were most unbecoming in shorts.

"Merry Christmas, Mrs. Stevens." He tipped his hat. "You've got a package that won't fit in your box. Thought I'd bring your mail up to you."

She took the parcel from him. "That's kind of you, Henry. I appreciate it very much."

He tugged the bill of his cap. "You have a nice day, you hear."

Back inside, with the box balanced on her hip, Eleanor searched through her writing desk for her good scissors. Unable to find them, she went to the kitchen where the aromas of ginger and cinnamon lingered in the air. Years ago, Isabel and she had stopped exchanging Christmas gifts, but gingerbread cookies were Isabel's favorites, and Eleanor had to give her something. Sorting through her sundries drawer, she found her kitchen scissors and used them to open the box, which held three books the members of her book club planned to read. There was a murder mystery, written by a friend of her daughter's, a best-seller by a relative of Isabel's who lived in Moncks Corner, and a romance novel, which one of the members assured everyone was minus any tawdry and totally unnecessary-to-the-story sexual encounters. The group, which had been meeting for fifty years, was nothing if not eclectic, Eleanor admitted.

Soon, she settled back in her Laura Ashley chair and immersed herself in the mystery novel, stopping once in a while to nibble a cookie and take a sip of eggnog. Isabel often criticized Eleanor's recipe, saying it had more egg than nog, but it suited Eleanor just fine.

Later that evening, after eating a bowl of vegetable soup and cornbread, Eleanor took her bath, dressed in her powder-blue silk pajamas, and slipped into bed. Propped up on three pillows, she read the mystery novel until her eyelids grew heavy. She roused herself from her stupor long enough to offer a short prayer.

Lord, I thank you for this day and for helpful, caring friends. And Lord, it's such a little thing, but could I have Boaz back? I really don't want to spend the money to buy a new one. In Jesus precious name, amen.

Just as she was about to fall asleep, she felt a niggling itch in the middle of her back. Searching the covers for her backscratcher, she wondered if she should have asked the Lord why He couldn't make her back itch in a place where she could reach it.

The next morning, as Eleanor was leaving for church, she opened the door to find her neighbor, Claudia, poised to knock.

"Mornin'," Claudia greeted cheerfully. "Harry and I thought we'd give you a ride to Sunday school." She held out her arm, crooked at the elbow as if to lend support.

"Well, all right. That's very thoughtful of you."

When they arrived at the church, Harry helped her up the steps and escorted her to her classroom.

During the few minutes between Sunday school and the eleven o'clock service, the president of the JOY Class (Jesus first, Others second and You last), walked Eleanor to the elevator and seated her in the sanctuary. Looking around, she admired the Frazier fur Christmas wreaths in the windows and the rows of potted poinsettias lined across the steps in front of the lectern. She searched down the list of names in the program until she found hers indicating that she had bought two of the poinsettias.

During the organ prelude, Isabel slipped into the pew beside her, wafting a cloud of Shalimar perfume all about them. She patted Eleanor on her leg. "I sent up a little prayah for you this mornin'. Take heart, Sugah, the Lord always comes through and makes our lemons into lemonade."

Eleanor blanched and braced herself for the lightning she felt might strike their pew. *Bless her, she may have her theological metaphors mixed up, but her heart's in the right place.*

Later that afternoon, after Eleanor had eaten a bowl of chicken noodle soup and had settled herself down to read, the doorbell rang again.

A young woman in her twenties stood on the doorstep, smiling brightly. "Mrs. Stevens?"

"Yes."

The woman turned and waved to a man and a little boy waiting at the end of the sidewalk. "It's the right place," she called out to them.

"Mrs. Stevens, I'm Sara Walker and this is my husband, Bobby, and our son, Bobby Junior. I think we have something that belongs to you."

Eleanor looked at the boy, who may have been five or six years old, and realized he was carrying *Boaz*. He walked up to her and with a solemn look, offered her the cane.

"Why, thank you so much, young man. I've been looking for this." She propped it against the wall.

The boy stepped back behind his mama and peeked around her skirt.

"I'm afraid I must apologize for not returning this sooner—" Mrs. Walker began.

"Please, won't you come in?"

"No thanks, really. We need to get back home. But I just have to tell you about finding this. It was nothing short of a miracle."

"A miracle?" asked Eleanor.

"Yes, you see, Bobby Junior, here, was supposed to be a shepherd in his Christmas play this morning in Sunday school—"

"One of the shepherds biting in the fields," interrupted Bobby Junior.

Mrs. Walker patted her son's head. "But as things would have it, we were runnin' late. And halfway to the church, he yells out that he had forgotten his shepherd's crook. I told him it was too late to turn back, and he started havin' a hissy-fit. Crying like you wouldn't believe. I tried to tell him he'd be just fine, but he wasn't havin' any of it. So, I just lifted up a prayer and asked the Lord to help us out.

"Next thing you know we're almost at the Piggly Wiggly, and Bobby Junior yells out, 'Look there! It's a shepherd's crook!'"

Eleanor pressed her hand to her heart.

"Sure enough, off to the side of the road was your cane. I hope you don't mind that we borrowed it for a while. But it sure was an answer to my prayer."

"That's quite a story. But I'm happy things turned out so well for all of us."

"Yes, ma'am." Mrs. Walker pulled Bobby Junior from behind her. "Tell Mrs. Stevens thank you."

"Thank you, ma'am."

"You're most welcome."

"I guess we better be getting' on," said Mrs. Walker.

Eleanor watched the three of them walk down her sidewalk, get in their car, and drive away. Shaking her head, she picked up *Boaz* and went inside.

Thank you, Lord, for the little things, she prayed. *Now, if I could just find my backscratcher.*

About the Author

Susan F. Craft is retired from a 45-year career as a writer for public television, a communications director for a state agency, a pharmacy continuing education planner for a university, and a proofreader for the SC Senate. An admitted history nerd, she enjoys painting, singing, listening to music, and sitting on her front porch watching rabbits eat all her daily lily bulbs. In 2011, Susan's Revolutionary War romantic suspense, *The Chamomile*, won the SIBA Okra Pick. She is represented by Linda S. Glaz, Hartline Literary Agency.

On January 12, 2015, Lighthouse Publishing of the Carolinas will release Susan's post-Revolutionary War suspense novel, entitled *Laurel*.

You can find Susan online at:

Website: www.susanfcraft.com

Historical Fiction a Light in Time:

http://historicalfictionalightintime.blogspot.com

Colonial Quills: http://colonialquills.blogspot.com

Stitches Thru Time: http://stitchesthrutime.blogspot.com

Heroes, Heroines and History: http://www.hhhistory.com

Banking on Christmas

KARLA AKINS

"I hear you have a blast on Christmas Eve, Eleanor. Everyone's told me how you go all out."

Eleanor nodded as she counted out the last of her cash and wrote down the amount of cash in her drawer. "I won't trade that night for anything." She smiled thinking of her little ones' excitement at Christmas.

June slammed her money drawer shut and locked it. "I thought moving to this small town would be a bore, but getting to know you this past year has been a treat." She grabbed her coat off the wall, wrapped an ugly red and green scarf around her neck and shuffled to the exit. "You about ready to go? I'll walk you to the car if you want."

"Nah. I'm short two cents and need to recount."

June shrugged. "If you say so. Merry Christmas!" She pushed the door open and bumped into a large man in a red suit. "Excuse me, sir, we're closed."

"I'm here to see Eleanor."

Eleanor looked up from counting. "Chris! Come on in. It's okay, June. Lock us in, will you?"

"Sure thing. Merry Christmas!" June waved and locked the door behind her.

Eleanor smiled at the visitor. "What brings you here so late? I figured you'd be booked the rest of the day since it's Christmas Eve."

"I am. I am. Just need a little favor." A gun snaked out from a cloud of white fur at the edge of his long red sleeve.

"What are you doing?"

"What does it look like?"

"But…but you're Santa. You can't rob a bank."

"Santa isn't real."

"Yes he is. What will children think if they watch the news and find out Santa robbed a bank? On Christmas Eve?"

"Shut up and let me inside the vault."

"Why?"

"You'll see."

Eleanor pointed her chin at him. "I don't know the combination."

"You don't need one. You have clearance. Swipe your I.D."

Eleanor grabbed the I.D. on the lanyard around her neck. "How did you know?"

"I've been watching you, Eleanor."

Eleanor gasped. "That proves you really are Santa. Santa watches everything we do."

"Move it." He gestured to the vault.

"Gee, I didn't know Santa was so grumpy." Eleanor walked to the vault and swiped her card. "It won't open, see?"

"You know you have to enter a number manually. Do it."

"I don't like your attitude."

"Yeah, well, I'm the one with the gun, remember?"

"You won't get by with this." She pointed to the surveillance cameras.

"I cut the lines."

She glared at him and turned to enter a password on the digital display. A motor whirred and the vault clicked open.

He motioned with his gun. "Move it."

"I didn't know Santa was so pushy, either."

"But you were expecting me, Eleanor. You always expect me on Christmas Eve. Did you set out those special macadamia nut cookies for me this year?"

"I haven't been home yet. If you let me go, I can make sure they're ready for you."

"First things first. Open it."

"Which one?"

"122413"

"I don't have a key."

"Yes you do. I know where you keep it. And you don't want me going after it."

Eleanor scowled. "If you're Santa, who makes sure you're naughty or nice? You don't deserve anything for Christmas." She reached inside her sweater and pulled out a key to unlock the door.

"Hurry up."

She turned the key, slid the cold steel box out of its hiding place and sat it on a table.

Santa pointed his gun at her. "Open it."

"Are you sure you want me to? You do know what's inside right?"

Santa nodded.

She opened it slowly.

Santa smiled. "Perfect."

"You like it?"

Santa held up the fishing lure. "I love it. It's exactly what I wanted." He leaned over the table and kissed Eleanor full on the mouth.

Eleanor giggled. "Oh, Chris, this was the best Christmas Eve role play yet. What will we do next year to top it?"

"I was thinking maybe a home robbery."

"We did that in 2009, remember?"

"Oh yeah." Chris shrugged. "I'm sure you'll come up with something. Did you really make my favorite cookies?"

"I did."

"We better hurry home to the kids. They'll wonder where Mom and Dad are on Christmas Eve." They locked up the vault and Eleanor returned the keys to the safe under the counter. She turned to Chris and slid into his arms. "You're such a good Santa. Merry Christmas, Mr. Claus."

"Merry Christmas, Mrs. Claus. Let's give the bank manager something to talk about."

Moving in front of the surveillance camera, they kissed.

And Eleanor shot the camera a big thumbs up.

About the Author

Karla Akins is an award-winning, prolific writer of books, short stories, plays, poems, songs, and countless nonfiction articles. Her biography of *Jacques Cartier* went #1 in its category on Amazon.

Besides writing biographies and history books for middle grades, she also writes fiction. Her first fiction novel, *The Pastor's Wife Wears Biker Boots* was released in 2013. Her short stories have been published in four *Splickety Magazine* editions. She is an online columnist for Examiner.com acting as the National History Examiner, National Special Needs Kids Examiner, National Homeschool Examiner, Fort Wayne Homeschool Examiner and Fort Wayne Preppers Examiner. She blogs at her website and on her History Scroll blog that interacts with the history books she writes for middle grades. Karla also engages her readers regularly via her website, and social media platforms such as Facebook, twitter, Pinterest, LinkedIn, tumblr and google+.

She is a classically trained musician on piano, violin and voice as well as a bible scholar. She earned her seminary degrees at Kingsway Theological Seminary including a bachelor's degree in Pastoral Theology, and a master's and doctorate in Christian Education.

Karla is also a pastor's wife, mother of five, and grandma to seven beautiful little girls. She lives in Northeast Indiana with her husband, twin teenage boys with autism, mother-in-law with Alzheimer's and three rambunctious dogs. When she's not writing she's riding her motorcycle, taking pictures, and looking for ancient treasure.

You've finished. Before you go…
Tweet/share that you finished this book
Rate this book.

17336511R00110

Made in the USA
Middletown, DE
27 November 2018